RETURN OF THE SHADOWS
Book 1

DONALD L. MARINO

PAGE PUBLISHING, INC.
New York, NY

First originally published by Page Publishing, Inc. 2018

ISBN 978-1-64138-797-2 (Paperback)
ISBN 978-1-64138-799-6 (Hardcover)
ISBN 978-1-64138-798-9 (Digital)

Printed in the United States of America

PROLOGUE

Ayre sat in a chair in his library. He had selected a book from the many that surrounded him; it was one on the history of the elves. As the king, he knew it well, but something was nagging at him and he wasn't sure what it was. His long, slender frame now relaxed in his chair. He had his long blond hair pulled back and tied at the back of his head, revealing his long pointed ears. He thumbed through the book, hoping something would jump out at him, but nothing had so far. Then suddenly, he felt a presence. He tensed and reached for the short sword that was attached to the side of the chair.

"Is that how you great an old friend?"

It was a familiar voice that brought relief.

"Alastrine, only you could get past the guards." Ayre relaxed

Alastrine smiled as he stepped into the light and pulled the hood of his cloak back. His short black hair a mess from the hood but the rest of him as neat as ever. A well-trimmed goatee. His well-built six-foot-plus frame stood in black boots. He wore lightweight pants and shirt under his cloak that protected him well. Every keeper had it, a gift from the goddess to keep them safe.

"Well, I assume this is not a social visit. Creeping in so no one knows you are here. Me feeling the need to read history." He gestured toward the book that lay on the table beside the chair he was sitting in.

"I'm afraid you are right, old friend." The smile he had at seeing his old friend faded.

"Yes, well, as you are the keeper, my fears of late must be right."

Alastrine was the keeper of the magic that saved the lands and the four races centuries ago. At that time, humans ruled the majority of the lands, which spread out over the oceans. Their greed, hatred, and negative ways enabled Goddess Hel, ruler of the underworld, to let shadow creatures loose on the world. They would suck the soul right out of living beings and use it to make them stronger, or they would inhabit weaker-minded creatures and use them for their bidding, which they did with the trolls. They had them go to war with the other four races—the dwarfs, elves, hawk people, and the humans. They were able to drive the few who survived to one island where the leaders go together and ask Goddess Atla, Hel's sister, for help. She ruled over water, healing, love, and health. She had them go to the waterfalls that ran off a plateau and instructed the humans and dwarfs to put short swords in the water. Then she told the elves and hawk people to put bows in the water. She picked someone to use each of these items and called them the proctors. Then she gave a green gem to the dwarfs and said it represented earth. Then a yellow one to the hawk people and said it represented air. Then a red one to the humans and said it represented fire, and finally a blue one to the elves and said it represented water. She then picked someone to use each of these items and called them the wielders. When the stones were correctly used, their energy was sent into a large crystal that was able to disperse that energy around the world, restoring balance. The trolls had fled as the shadows were no longer directing them and the war was over. What remained of the four races decided to stay on the island as the rest of the world was not safe. The hawk people took a small island off the coast of the big one. The humans went west and the dwarfs went north. The elves stayed close to the falls and built a temple to house the crystal. What remained of the trolls fled into the rocky cliffs so as not to be seen. The goddess now picked a keeper for the magical items until they were needed again. For their service, they were granted a long life. In the seven centuries since, there have only been seven keepers—one dwarf, one hawk person, two humans, and two elves. Alastrine was the second human and only had been the keeper for a short time.

"The shadows are back. Things in the human lands are bad. Greed, hate, they're all on the rise," Alastrine said sadly.

"I know, I keep watch. The hawk people are struggling ever since Mir was killed and his son took over head of council. The dwarfs, well, they have always been short-tempered. It just seems worse now."

"And here?"

"We feel it here too." Alastrine snickered a little, knowing elves don't like to admit they have problems.

"No, we do, little minor things get blown up into big things. I see it, but many do not. We try and do what we can to calm it down. It doesn't always work." He looked at Alastrine, now concern showing in his blue eyes. "So back to your visit."

Alastrine pulled a bow and a bag with the blue gem in it from under his cloak.

"I see, and whom do I bestow this great responsibility on?" he asked as he took them and placed them on the table by the chair he was sitting on.

Alastrine handed him a sealed envelope. "On the second full moon from tonight, open this to see the names."

He took the envelope and looked at it questioningly.

"This is the goddess's instructions. I will be tied up in the human lands by then." He nodded and said nothing.

"The rest will gather at the temple. The magic needs to take place by the falls. I'm sorry, my friend, I wish I had time to catch up more, but I must go." With that, he pulled his hood up and disappeared back into the darkness.

Ayre was left standing there, holding the envelope. Wondering whose names he was holding.

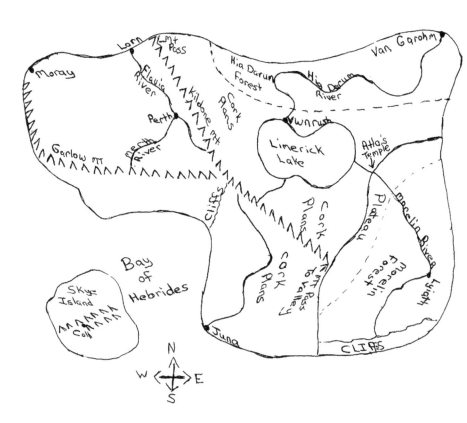

CHAPTER 1

He had been walking for hours through the misty afternoon and into the evening. His long, black hair, now soaked, once again fell into his eyes, and he brushed it back and slipped on the wet stones. His short, slender frame was already saturated, and he had now caught a chill. It had been drizzling and raining all day, and even though it was mostly flat in the part of the land, everything was wet, muddy, and slippery.

His thoughts drifted, and he slipped on the wet stones and, this time, went face-first into a mud puddle. He rolled over and sat back into another puddle. He wiped the mud from his eyes the best he could.

"Rain or don't rain, just do it and be done already!" he yelled to the sky.

He stood and brushed his tattered clothes off as much as he could, then he looked down at the odd leather bag at his side. Black leather stitched together with red thread. He shifted the strap on his shoulder, and the weight of whatever was inside shifted as well.

"Take this and go to the elves," Alastrine had told him. "Do not open it for any reason."

"Why? What is it?" he had asked.

"You will find out when you need to know." Alastrine's big frame loomed over him.

"OK" was all he could say, not sure that he should ask any other questions.

"Listen to me." Alastrine held his shoulders and looked into his eyes. "The goddess has picked you for this. She has great faith in you, and so do I. It is time for you to go. It is not safe here anymore. Be careful and may the goddess bless you."

"OK," he had responded, but very confused. He turned and started to walk out the east gate of Moray.

"Two others will meet up with you in the morning."

He looked back, gave a weak smile, and continued to walk. That was early afternoon, and now dusk was coming.

"Elves!" he said as he brushed his hair away again. "They haven't talked to humans for centuries." He muttered in frustration as he slipped on another stone. He caught himself this time and slowly started walking again.

"What if they lock me up?" he thought out loud.

"A lot depends on you," Alastrine had told him.

"Why me?" he yelled out loud.

"You have been chosen by the goddess." Alastrine's voice came in his head again.

"Chosen for what?" he said, knowing no answer was coming. He stopped walking. He was soaked to the bone, chilled, and tired. Tears started to fill his eyes.

"I don't understand what I'm doing." He hung his head for a few moments. Then he took a deep breath, wiped away the tear, rain mixture from his eyes.

"It's not safe here." Alastrine's voice came in his head again.

"Why? What's after me? What did I do?" Tears started to come again, and his stomach was in knots. "Why did the goddess pick me? I'm just an orphan boy who gets by, by doing odd jobs. I'm no one special," he muttered to himself.

"The goddess has faith in you and so do I" came Alastrine's voice again.

"Faith in me for what?" He threw his hands in the air.

He slipped again and almost went down. His hand brushed against the leather bag he carried, and he looked at it.

"Do not open the bag or touch what is inside," Alastrine had told him when he gave him the bag.

"What is so important that I have to carry it but can't touch it? Why am I doing this?" Tears started to come again. His body chilled, soaked and tired from walking all afternoon, and now the rain started to fall harder, and he was having trouble seeing and slipped and fell backward into a puddle, knocking the wind out of him. Now he let the tears flow freely. Frustration and exhaustion over took him.

He looked up, and in the woods, just off the path, stood the biggest buck he had ever seen. He wiped his eyes to get a better look, and the buck was looking right at him. Then he thought he was going crazy, but it looked like the buck wanted him to follow him.

"May the goddess bless you," Alastrine's voice came again.

"Goddess, did you send him?" he asked hopefully

The buck looked at him, then into the woods again.

He got up and slowly followed the buck. It led him to a place where several thick pine trees stood by a large boulder. It was mostly dry underneath, and the old needles were a nice soft place to lie down, which he did and was soon fast asleep.

* * * * *

Alastrine watched as Whiley walked through the east gate and into the mist, and shortly he was out of sight. His brown eyes betrayed his hard look. He was very concerned about the young man.

"He will be fine." A soft voice came in his head.

"My lady," Alastrine replied as he always did when the goddess talked to him.

"I can protect the boy better out of the city. My sister has more control here. The negativity of the humans has given her power," the goddess tried to comfort him.

"I know, my lady. I feel I should have told him more."

"He isn't ready. You did the right thing."

"I hope so." Alastrine turned to head into town.

"Felix, glad you came," Alastrine said after a few steps.

"You are the only human that can sense my presence."

A wood sprite flew out in front of him. He had red hair and green eyes. He was only six inches tall and had wings as big as his body, and he wore a green tunic.

"You need my help?" He smiled.

"Yes." Alastrine half answered, his thoughts still on Whiley.

"What's wrong? You're far away." Felix was concerned.

"I have sent the wielder, a boy, to the elves." Alastrine stopped walking.

"You need me for?"

"I need you to go with him. Watch over him and the other boy."

"It's a long trip."

"It's coming fast. Time is short."

"Where is he?"

"I sent him on his way a short time ago. It was not safe for him here. Just follow him tonight. I told him others would be joining him in the morning."

"I will get them there safe."

"You need to meet up with the dwarfs in Vwnrugh at the west gate. Nonmumi will be looking for you. Then proceed to the temple."

"Then off I go." He turned and flew out of sight.

Alastrine stood, thinking about what was coming. Many lives will be lost. He shook his head sadly.

"Alastrine, sir," a voice came through the mist. Alastrine shook his head, clearing his thoughts to see a young man coming toward him.

"Leigh, glad to see you back safe."

A young man emerged from the mist. He was average height with light brown hair and brown eyes. He was medium built and very fit. His clothes were rags at best, but his personality was always upbeat and happy.

"Alastrine, sir, I delivered the messages and items to the dwarfs and hawk people," Leigh reported, wiping the rain out of his eyes. "They were disappointed it wasn't you, but they understood."

"They will send the chosen ones?" Alastrine asked.

"The dwarfs cursed the humans, but said they would," Leigh hesitated.

"And the hawk people?"

Leigh took a deep breath. He had been with Alastrine a long time—doing odd and end jobs and, from time to time, running messages—and he knew he was going to be angry at what he had to tell him.

"The leader of the council was not happy that his son was not chosen as the protector. So there was an argument about who should go."

"Fools!" Alastrine spat. Leigh stepped back. "How dare he question the goddess. Time is short. They better do the right thing."

He looked back a Leigh, who looked ready to run.

"What of the trolls? Did you notice anything?" His voice softened now.

"They seem more organized than I have ever seen them," Leigh reported.

"The shadows," Alastrine muttered to himself. "OK, you have the sword I gave you?"

"Of course." Leigh smiled. He had been thrilled when Alastrine told him the goddess chose him as the human protector. He had spent the next morning reading the history to understand what his role was.

"The wielder had been chosen, and I have sent him on his way already." Alastrine smiled.

"Him?" Leigh was surprised; most wielders were female because they are more nurturing. Well, at least that is what he thought, but no one knew for sure except for the goddess.

"Yes, Whiley was chosen."

"My Whiley?" Leigh's eyes lit up. Even through the rain, Alastrine could see that.

"Yes, Felix, a wood sprite, is following him, and you need to catch up by morning."

"Yes, sir," Leigh said with a lot of excitement in his voice.

"He doesn't know the history or what he has been chosen for. Explain it to him a little at a time. Don't overwhelm him. Be smart and stay safe. May the goddess bless you."

Alastrine patted him on the back as he sent him out of the east gate.

CHAPTER 2

Alastrine walked into the city. It was early afternoon, and although the rain had kept some people in, the streets were still busy with people selling and buying a variety of items. Most days there was a lot of small talking going on as well, but not today; it was too damp and cold. Fall was coming, and you could feel it in the air.

Alastrine walked down several narrow streets, his face buried deep in his hood. His thoughts in a million different places at the same time. Were the races ready to battle for their existence? He wasn't sure about that. So much hate and only caring about one's self is going on right now. Caring for the greater good seemed to be a thing of the past.

Could the chosen ones use to stones and the crystal to bring balance back? He knew all the chosen and felt good about them, but this was a big task.

He was now standing at the door of a small house that had a tiny alleyway. He took a look inside his home, understanding what it was that they needed to do and would they be able to do it.

He opened the door, and the three men sitting at his table looked at him. They were all dressed well and looked very anxious

They were the governors at the three human cities. Scott from Lorn, the oldest and largest of the cities. Scott was a stocky man with all the muscles from his days as a logger. He had short brown hair and brown eyes.

There was Alex from Morey. Morey was the second largest city. Alex was a tall, slender man with red hair and beard. He had green eyes that could make anyone weak in the knees.

There was Roger from Perth. Perth was the youngest and smallest of the cities but the fastest growing. Roger was slim and short with black hair and goatee. He had brown puppy eyes that made it hard for anyone to say no to him.

"Why have you ask us here?" Alex asked as they stood to greet him. They all knew and had great respect for Alastrine. So when he asked for a meeting, none of them hesitated.

Alastrine lowered his hood, and the three standing there could tell by the look in his face that this was not good news he had to share.

"The chosen have been picked and are on their way to the temple. The elves will help using the stones and crystal to restore the balance," Alastrine said in a low voice.

The three slowly sat down, not sure what to day or do.

"Rumors have been filtering into the city of cattle being found dead, but no signs of how they died," Roger slowly said.

"The shadows are returning. They steal souls and use weak-minded creatures to do their bidding," Alastrine said, slowly letting what he was saying sink in.

"The trolls," Roger blurted out. "They have been seen in the lower mountain area. They don't usually come so far down."

They all looked at Alastrine.

"This is why I have called you here. Dark times are coming. We need to be ready," Alastrine said, looking from face to face.

"What should we do?" Scott asked.

"Go back to your cities, ready your city for what's to come. Fortify your walls, have evacuation plans for everyone. People will be coming in from the countryside as the trolls come. Keep things as calm as you can. Fear only feeds the shadows. Stock up on supplies. You will need them. Have blessed water. It will slow them down. Time is short, my friends, so act quickly, and may the goddess bless us."

Alastrine stepped away from the door. The three knew that meant the meeting was over. They slowly stood and left without a word.

* * * * *

A small sailboat bobbed up and down in the choppy waters of the Bay of Hebrides. Three hawk people were on board, on their way to Juna and then onto the temple.

Hawk people had white wings with brown spots and a black or brown beck for a nose. Other than that, they looked human.

A muscular hawk person, Rex, sat in the middle of the boat, hovering over a small framed hawk girl in front of him. Rex had blond hair and blue eyes and black beck. He thought he was better than everyone else and didn't hide that he felt that way.

"Now, Lora, remember the council said for you to carry the stone, but when it comes time to use it, I will be the one wielding it." Rex puffed his chest up to make himself look bigger.

Lora was the small framed girl who sat in front of him. She had a brown beck and green eyes and long sandy blond hair. She was very quiet and shy, but her facial expression told how sick she was of hearing Rex tell her over and over how he was going to wield the stone. She put her hand on the brown leather bag that was sewn with yellow thread and wondered anew why she was chosen

"Rex, that is not what they said," came a voice from behind him. "They said if she couldn't wield it that I let you try."

"Tanner, you really think she can handle magic of this kind?" Rex laughed.

Tanner was a little smaller than Rex, but not by much. He had a brown beck hair and eyes. His hair was short and curly.

"She was chosen by the goddess as was I. I'm not about to question the goddess, are you?" Tanner snapped back as he worked the sail.

Lora smiled to herself. *He is cute and comes to my rescue*, she thought to herself.

"We should have just flown over," Rex muttered as the boat hit more rough waters.

"The council said that was too risky. We need to keep a low profile and get to the temple as fast as we can," Tanner reminded him.

"Staying close to the water keeps us close to the goddess." Lora smiled as she watched some dolphins swim by.

"All I need is me." Rex puffed himself up again.

Tanner and Lora both rolled their eyes.

"Juna, just ahead." Tanner pointed at the docks that looked very small in the distance.

"Remember, when we get there, it will be dusk. We move fast through the city and keep a low profile," Tanner said as he adjusted the sail to head toward the docks.

* * * * *

The hawk council gathered the afternoon that the trio left for the temple. Rumors had been flying around since Leigh had delivered the message from Alastrine. Humans didn't ever come to the island, and now three hawk people were seen leaving in a sailboat. The council wanted to stop fear from spreading because it would only feed the shadows. The council members had gathered in a small meeting room off the main hall. They could hear the main hall filling up as voices got louder and louder.

"Now remember, I will do the talking. In times like this, there needs to be one strong voice to lead," Lor said.

Lor was Rex's father. He stood over six feet tall with a black beck, long light brown hair, and green eyes.

"As I am high minister, it is my duty to make my subjects feel safe."

"Lor, as council members, we all have a right to speak," Lark countered.

Lark was the oldest council member. He was only five and half foot tall with black beck and hair that was cut short, with brown eyes. He didn't let anyone intimidate him for any reason.

Lor turned and opened the door and entered the main hall, ignoring Lark. The rest of the council followed him out and took their places at the council table that faced the standing room-only crowd.

Lor stood and motioned for everyone to sit and quiet down.

"I want to calm everyone. My son, Rex, and two others have gone to see if there is anything to be concerned about. If there is, Rex will take care of it." His arrogance filled the room as he spoke.

"Then why are soldiers being sent to the outer towers of the island?" a voice came from the crowd.

Lark went to talk but was cut off by Lor.

"The council feels it will make everyone feel safer, but Rex will take care of anything before it gets here."

A murmur went through the crowd.

"The army has scheduled a lot of training, why?" another voice came.

"All just precautions." Lor motioned for quiet again. "We are very safe here on our island. I beg you to go home and carry on your normal routine. All is fine." With that he pounded his gavel and ended the meeting. The hall slowly emptied. Lor shook hands and talked to some as they left. Many, however, didn't like or trust him and wished his father, Mir, was still alive.

Mir had been high minister for a long time. He was kind and humble. He would ask for input from the council and others. Lor took over his place several months ago when his father was murdered. The murder was still unsolved, and many questioned if Lor was involved. Lor had become a bully with the council from day one. The council finally stood up to him over his son being the wielder but ended up agreeing to let him go along.

The eight council members had gathered to one side of the hall and stopped Lor as he was about to leave.

"You are crossing a line, Lor. You are not a king or anything close. We are getting tired of your attitude and the way you dismiss us. Be careful. There are ways to have you removed," Lark spat a Lor.

"You wouldn't dare. The public loves me. They wouldn't stand for it." Lor was smug.

"They loved your father. They tolerate you. That won't last forever." With that, Lark turned and left, followed by the rest of the council.

Lor watched them leave, knowing he was right, and decided he needed to act to prevent that from happening.

CHAPTER 3

The dwarf council of elders acted immediately upon receiving Alastrine's message. The chosen had been summoned to the great tree. This was an apple tree that was several hundred years old. The five elders each had a seat carved into it. They were the only ones allowed to eat the apples from the tree as it was said to give them wisdom that helped rule the dwarfs.

Dagnel had been chosen as the protector. The elders all agreed it was a good choice. Dagnel was four and half feet tall. His long brown hair was pulled back into a ponytail. He had brown eyes and a goatee. He wore a leather cover on his head and leather boots. His clothes were leather as well. He carried a short sword, the sword Alastrine sent for him.

Alastrine was the chosen wielder. She stood four foot two, her red hair pulled to the sides and braided. She had green eyes, and her clothes were plain and much lighter. She did wear leather boots. She had a short sword and a leather bag sewed with green thread that held the stone. The elders were very happy with this choice.

The elder in the center seat stood.

"The goddess had picked the chosen once more, and once more we are sending two of our own to help restore the balance. Dagrel and Arastrude, may the goddess be with you," the elder said to the small crowd that had gathered. "We send you off with one of our best soldiers who will guide you safely to the temple." The elder gestured to his left, and a middle-aged dwarf stepped forward. "This is Nonmumi. May the goddess bless all of you." With that, the elders got up and left.

Nonmumi stood four feet eight. He had black hair and beard both tied into ponytails. He had brown eyes and wore a metal helmet to hide his thinning hair. Nonmumi was a good tracker and fighter. He spent many years serving in the army. He carried his favorite weapon—a battle ax.

He was very straight to the point and didn't have time for nonsense.

They said their goodbyes and left the capital city of Von Garohm. They were going to Vwnrugh to meet up with the humans, then go to the temple.

The morning was sunny and warm as they left.

"Calm before the storm," Nonmumi muttered as he led the way.

"Are we following the river?" Arastrude asked.

"Not too easy for the shadows to find us. At midday tomorrow, we will leave the river path and go on the old trail through the woods," Nonmumi barked.

"Are we sure the humans will be there?" Dagnel asked.

Nonmumi, already tired of the questions, rolled his eyes.

"Well, Felix knows we will be looking for them. He is very reliable." Nonmumi walked faster now, and they both got the feeling he was over the questions.

They followed the river path. The path followed the Hia Darum River. Merchants used it, as well as boats on the river, to get good from Von Garohm to Vwnrush and back. There were many rest stations along the way; they offered cabins available for the night. It was close to fall, but the forest that butted the trails on the other side was still lush and green. It made for a beautiful walk.

As they walked, many hunters, fishers, and merchants passed by with no more than a wave. They stopped midday and ate a light lunch of cheese and dried fruit.

"We need to move on. We have to make it to the campsite by nightfall." Nonmumi got up and started off again, not waiting for them. They looked at each other, jumped up, and ran after him.

The afternoon stayed sunny and warm, and as they kept moving, Dagrel and Arastrude became more relaxed. They chatted back and forth about idle stuff to pass time. They talked about things they enjoyed doing and training they had gone through and laughed at silly things they had done.

Nonmumi stayed ahead of them and kept quiet, but he could hear them, and it was slowly making him crazy. Finally, Nonmumi turned with his battle ax and put it into the ground right in front of them. He was so fast they didn't have time to react.

"This is not a picnic or afternoon stroll. This is real, and you need to pay attention to what is going on around you and shut your traps. The goddess put great faith in you. Don't let her down." With that, he pulled his ax up, turned, and walked on.

The two stood in shock for a moment. Then Arastrude went to say something, but Dagnel grabbed her arm. Then they both just followed quietly.

* * * * *

Lotgren had been placed in charge of the dwarf army several years ago by the elders. He was a big dwarf with black hair and a big, black mustache. He was well versed in many forms of combat and much older than those he commanded. Several younger dwarfs had challenged him and were sorry they did so. Until now, he had only done drills and training, but now it was real. Trouble was coming, most likely by the trolls. He had never seen one but knew how big they were and how hard it was going to be to defeat them.

He was standing, watching two young dwarfs talking as they packed their bags to head out to the defensive lines at the edge of the forest. He turned and looked at the door in front of him. His four commanders sat inside, waiting for him. He took a deep breath and opened the door.

"Gentlemen." The four stood. "Please have a seat." He looked around the room.

There was Bhargel. He was a young burly commander with red hair that matched his fiery temper. He was just promoted two years ago and was already highly respected by his troops.

There was Deptoe. He was the oldest of the commanders. His black hair had white hair showing through. He was looking forward to retiring in a couple of years.

There was Brakac. His father had been a commander, so Brakac was following in his footsteps and was very proud to do so. His brown hair and beard framed his face so only his eyes could really be seen.

Then there was Doggad. He was the quiet one. He would sit back, listen, and take everything in before saying anything. His long black hair hung halfway down his back.

"Gentlemen, I'm going to give details to you. They do not leave this room. I don't want fear to spread. It will make things worse."

The four were sitting already, having an idea of what he was going to say.

"The balance has been tipped. The shadows are back. The chosen ones have been picked and are on their way to the temple. Nonmumi is with them."

He took a deep breath to give each of them a moment to take in what he just said.

"Bhargel, I'm sending your division to the east. Start at the coast and come west. Take a small party and send to the temple to help the elves protect the crystal."

"Yes, sir."

"Deptoe, your division will start where Bhargel ends and go to Vwnrush. Brakac, your division will start at Vwnrugh and go west, and, Doggad, you will start where Brakac ends and go to the ocean. We are pretty sure it will be trolls coming as that is what happened last time. Don't go head-to-head with them. Use hit and run."

There was a moment of silence

"Again, give little information. Tell them it's training. Fear feeds the shadows."

"Sir, what of the other races?" Brakac asked.

"The elves, I'm sure, are prepared. The hawk people, well, they are up in the air. The humans, rumors have it they are already having troll problems."

"Will the humans be coming this way, sir?" Bhargel asked.

"Most likely, but we need to be ready for anything. Gentlemen, you have your orders. May the goddess bless our task."

"Bless be," they all said. They got up and left as Lotgren watched them go.

He said under his breath, "Bless us, my lady."

CHAPTER 4

It was the second full moon since Alastrine had visited the elf king. Now Ayre walked in the garden at the palace. He loved being out here near nature when things stressed him.

He looked once again at the paper he held in his hand. He had opened the envelope only three hours ago and sent his personal page to get the two whose names were there.

Luvon was named as the protector. A boy just past his nineteenth summer, he had long blond hair and blue eyes. He lived on the outskirts of the city on a farm. He was a very talented hunter.

Elyon was named the wielder. She was just past her eighteenth summer. She had red hair and green eyes. She lived on the north side of the city where her parents had a bakery.

"Your Majesty," a voice broke his thoughts. "Sorry to bother you," Nasir, his personal page, said as he bowed.

Nasir was only past his fifteenth summer, but Ayre trusted him so that he hardly ever used any other page. He gave Nasir a room close to his so he was always near. Nasir had short red hair and green eyes.

"Nasir, are they here?" Ayre asked with a mix of emotions.

"Yes, Your Majesty." Nasir turned and motioned for them to come into the garden.

They entered slowly, not sure what was going on, only to be told the king wished to see them. They both stopped and bowed as the king came toward them but stayed silent as they were not sure of what to say or do.

"My friends, thank you for coming," Ayre said as he walked them into the garden. They both seemed to breathe a little easier as he had them sit at a small table, where drinks and fruits were waiting.

Ayre sat down and looked at the two across the table and wondered anew at how unfair it was to put so much on two that were so young.

"Please enjoy." Ayre motioned to the drinks and fruits. He took a drink himself, feeling very dry. He drank, then cleared his thought.

"I'm sure you are wondering why I have called you here. Well, the goddess and the elves have a need of your services."

They both looked confused.

"Your Majesty, what could I possibly do for the goddess and you?" Luvon asked softly.

"Do the two of you know the history of the war where the four races fought against the trolls and shadows, and the four races won with the help of the goddess?"

They both nodded slowly.

"Then you know about the keeper, protector, and wielder?"

Again, they both nodded.

"Well, the keeper was here, and things have become unbalanced. The shadows are in the lands again." He gestured to Nasir, who came with a bow and a leather bag sewed with the blue thread. He handed the bow to Luvon.

"Son, you have been chosen by the goddess as the protector."

He gave the bag to Elyon.

"And you, my dear, have been chosen by the goddess as the wielder."

They both took the items from him slowly, stunned at what was happening.

"I will have Captain Folmar take you to the temple by the falls. That is where the magic needs to happen. The others are on their way by now, I am sure. This is old magic, not elf magic. Be careful when using it. It will take a lot to succeed at what is being asked of you. I am sorry that you have not been given a choice in this but know that for your sacrifice, the elves will always be in your debt."

Ayre stopped talking to let what he had said sink in. Then he continued, "I know it's a lot, but time is short. I am sending tow guards home with each of you. Go, pack your supplies, say your farewells. Tell only whom you have to. The less that know, the better. We don't want fear to spread. It will only feed the shadows. You leave at dawn."

* * * * *

Whiley woke, slowly looking around, trying to remember how he got where he was. Then he remembered the deer and looked around quickly to see if he was still there.

"He already left," came a small voice, "when I got here to watch over you."

Whiley slid backward, looking around to see where the voice was coming from.

"I'm right here." And a six-inch creature flew out of the tree. "You were told about me."

"I was told I would meet up with two others today. I didn't know one would be a wood sprite." Whiley smiled at him.

He flew down in front of Whiley. "I'm Felix, and you are?" Felix stuck out his hand to shake.

"Felix, nice to meet you. I am Whiley." He stuck his pinky out to shake his hand.

"Good, now we need to get moving. We are wasting time we don't have."

The morning brought clearing, and the dampness faded away. The sun quickly dried his clothes as they walked. He felt better but kept looking at the bag on his side, wondering what it was for. He had thought maybe he should wait, maybe Felix had no idea.

"Where are we going?" Whiley finally asked.

"To the elves." Felix didn't even look back when answering.

"Why me?" he asked after a few moments.

"Excuse me?" This time, he glanced over his shoulder.

"Why did the goddess pick me?"

"I don't know. I don't question the goddess." He looked forward again and kept moving.

"You know a lot more than you're telling me, don't you?" he said as he followed him.

"I know more than you will ever know, but not to worry. You will learn things as you need to."

Whiley sighed and kept walking. The warm morning turned into an even warmer midday. They ate some berries, and Felix made sure no trace of their stop was left they moved on. After an hour of fast-paced moving, Whiley had enough.

"OK, I get that we are in a hurry, but I don't have wings, so can we slow the pace a little?"

"Sorry, my young friend. I want to be by the river by nightfall." He didn't slow his pace.

"Why do we need to be by the river by nightfall?" Whiley asked, trying to keep up.

"What?"

"Why do we need to be by the river by nightfall?"

"We just do."

"Is that where we are meeting the other person?"

"What other person?"

"The one that I was told about. I was told there would be two others meeting up with me."

"What? No. Your energy would be better used keeping up."

He sighed in frustration. He still knew nothing of what he was to do or why. He looked around him and realized something.

"Where is everyone?" he finally said.

"What now?" Felix was getting a little frustrated with all the questions.

"This path is always full of people going between the cities for one thing or another, but there is no one."

They both looked around for a moment.

"That's a good question for a change." He looked a moment longer. "I think we need to get off this road as soon as possible. I don't like this," Felix said.

"What does this mean?" Whiley asked, trying to keep up with the new faster pace.

"Bad things are coming, faster than what was expected, I am guessing. We need to get you to the elves."

"What bad things?"

"Things that no man alive has ever seen."

He stopped. "It's the shadows."

"Very good, now keep moving!" he yelled back at him.

His mind started racing. What was the history? He couldn't remember it at all. He stumbled as he ran.

"Whiley, Felix, wait up!" Leigh yelled as he was running to catch up.

"Where have you been?" Felix lashed out when he caught them.

"I followed your trail last night, Whiley, but when you went into the forest, there must have been a hundred deer following you, then erased all your tracks. Took me till now to catch up."

"Well, at least you're here," Felix muttered.

"There is more. Word has it that trolls are attacking farms at the base of the mountains. Farmers are starting to head for the cities for protection."

"Then let's keep moving. We need to be by the water by night-fall." Felix took off. The other two followed.

"Leigh, do you know why you are here?" Whiley asked, confused that Leigh was the other to show up. He knew him from around town, and he seemed like a good guy, but why did the goddess pick two kids off the streets?

"Yes, I'm the protector." Leigh smiled and kept running.

That answer confused him even more. And just then, they hit a split in the road. One way went to Lorn, the other to Perth.

"Which way?" Whiley asked, trying to catch his breath.

"Neither. We travel the fields for now. Try and stay out of sight," Leigh said.

"Good idea," Felix added.

CHAPTER 5

Roger left Moray early the next morning on his horse heading back to Perth. He had wanted to leave the night before, but Alex and Scott had asked him to stay. The three of them had sat up late, talking about what they thought might work to protect the cities and what to do if they needed to evacuate. They had agreed that Lorn should be the last stand. From there, they could escape of the mountains if need be.

The morning, unlike the night before, was clear and warm. He had left just as the city was waking up and people were going about business. He thought how things would change soon and wondered how the people would handle that change. Not good, he figured. Change never came easy or welcomed even if it was a good change. He waved at those he passed as he rode. It would be an all-day ride back to his city, Perth. He loved his city—so young and exciting like a teenager. Moray was nice but stuck and not growing happy where she was. Not Perth. It seemed its boarders kept growing every day. The thought of his city made him smile as he rode in the morning sun.

His horse came to an abrupt stop, bringing him out of his thoughts, and what he saw in front of him confused him. There were farmers with what looked like all their belongings they could carry on their wagons, with livestock following them. Children keeping chickens together and moving forward. Some of them were weeping. He rode up to the closest group.

"What is going on here?" he asked a man, who was walking two cows.

"The trolls, that's what," he answered, fighting back tears.

"What trolls?"

"The ones in the mountains. They come couple nights ago and attack our farms." His big eyes filled with tears now.

Roger looked around, and his heart sank. *They start already. Time is very short.*

"They didn't have to do what they did. I don't understand," the man continued.

"Do what?" Roger asked, coming back from his thoughts again.

"They tore my Lilly limb from limb." The tears flowed freely now.

He looked around the man and saw several children but no wife.

"She was rushing the children into the root cellar, and one of them came after them. She turned to take a stand." He could barely talk now.

"It's OK, sir. I understand," Roger tried to comfort him.

"She stabbed him twice with her sword, didn't even slow them down. They just ripped her to pieces like a rag doll." The man was sobbing now.

"If I may, sir, how did you end up here? I mean, where did the trolls go?"

"They flattened the house and the barn, killed a few animals, and went back into the mountains." The man looked at him like a small child to a parent. "Why did they do it? For what reason?"

Roger knew, of course, but didn't know what he should tell this poor man.

"I wish I had an answer for that, my friend. You have suffered a great deal, and for that I am sorry. Go to the city. They will help you as much as they can."

The man looked down to the ground like a child who had been told, "No, you can't stay up."

"I don't know what I am going to do without her, you know." With that, the man started walking again, followed by his children, with a wagon, a few belongings, and livestock.

Roger turned his horse and started riding hard; he had to get home. As he rode, he ran into more groups and was told more stories like the man's. Some said the shadows are back and that surprised him, but none understood why, and that was what they kept asking him—why are they doing this?

It was late afternoon, and he hadn't seen anyone for a long time. There should have been people going between the cities; this path was always busy. Then up ahead, he saw two boys going into the fields where the road splits. Then to his right, he noticed a horse coming fast from his city, and he rode to meet it.

"Sir, thank the goddess it's you. There are farmers moving into the city, telling stories of troll attacks. The city council sent me to find you. People of the city are ready to flee. Fear our wall won't keep them safe."

"Let's go then. We have a lot of work to do." The two hurried toward Perth.

* * * * *

Alastrine had just finished lunch and was looking through the history of the races again when a knock came at his door.

"Come in," he said, looking up from the book he was reading.

"Alastrine, Alex needs you at the south gate." It was Sherry, a pretty little woman with light brown hair and blue eyes. Alex and Sherry had been together for a long time, and they still were deeply in love. Today, her eyes showed distress and tears were starting to form.

"What it is, my dear?" Alastrine got up and went to her.

"Farmers coming, telling stories of troll attacks." She put her hand to her mouth to catch her breath.

"Take me to him." Alastrine and Sherry flew out of his house and down the small streets. The streets were abuzz with rumors of what was going on. Some shops were closing up, fearing the trolls weren't far behind. They soon arrived at the gate, and Alastrine was shocked at what he saw. Farmers with all the belongings they could carry, livestock, and children everywhere. He searched the crowd for Alex and saw him with a little old lady who was crying.

As he got closer, he could hear her story. "They just came from nowhere and broke down the doors. My son and husband went after them, and they grabbed them and ripped their arms and legs right off. It was awful. Their screams will never leave me." The woman was sobbing so hard it was hard to understand what she was saying. "We hid in the root cellar till we couldn't hear them anymore, then we grabbed what we could and came here."

Alex looked up at Alastrine. "I am hearing the same kind of stories over and over again. I didn't even get a chance to prepare for this." Alex was trying to keep himself together with all the grief going on around him.

"Alex, this is what we are going to do. First, I want messengers sent to Lorn and Perth. Tell them time is much shorter than we thought. I am sure they are starting to get them same as we are. Tell them not to waste time in getting all the plans that I ask for in place."

"I got just the guys for that." He turned and headed into town.

Alastrine turned to Sherry. "Sherry, honey, your help is needed as well. Take these people down by the dock, to the two old empty warehouses. That will at least give them shelter, and there is room there for the livestock. Get some of the ladies in town to help you with the bedding and food. Most importantly, just be there for them. Their grief is feeding the shadows. Anything we can do to ease that will help. I will be honest with you, my dear. Things will only get worse from here. We have a long road ahead of us."

"Alex has explained what is happening and what is coming. I will do whatever you need me to. I have a few women who are already here I can have help me. I will get more." She hugged Alastrine and left and went to a group of ladies who were hugging some of those who had just came into the gate.

"I have sent them on their way. What now?" Alex asked as he appeared through the crowd.

"I need nine bowmen and three men who are very creative and three boys to run messages."

"OK. What else?"

"Your wife is going to handle the people coming in. I am taking those I ask for and going to see what the trolls are doing and see if we can slow them down. I need you to secure the city. Make these walls stronger and build another one six feet or so in front. Prepare the women and children to move south when I say. If my guess is right, they will hit here first and move south across the land."

"That doesn't make me feel better." Alex swallowed hard.

"We will try and hold here as long as we can, have boats ready to carry the last from the city to Lorn when the city falls."

"Falls!"

"Listen, help will not make it here in time. Do as I say and save as many as we can. Have the people I need ready within the hour. I will meet all of you here."

Alex just stood; he was in shock at what he was hearing.

"Alex, I am sorry. I really am, but these are the facts we have to deal with. Now you need to lead this city. You have to pull it together."

"You're right. I'll be here with the men within the hour."

Alastrine left him to go get ready himself. He couldn't help but notice the tears in his eyes as he did so. The life Alex had known was ending, and he was trying to come to terms with that, like so many others would have to do. Alastrine wished there was more time for him to deal with it, but that was not possible. He worked on putting it out of his mind and on what needed to be done.

CHAPTER 6

The small boat docked at an end pier. They decided it would be best there so as not to draw any unwanted attention. It was one of the more shady areas of the city to enter from, but no one among them had ever left Skye Island before, and as they looked around, they knew why. Homeless lay sleeping by cans that had fires in them. It was getting late, and rats were sneaking around, looking for food the homeless didn't eat. The air was damp as it came off the bay, and many of the homeless only wore rags and lay by the cans, shivering as they tried to sleep. Lora wished she had blankets to give them. They were all quiet, not knowing what to say to each other. As they got closer to where people lived, their houses were going dark as the city went to bed.

"We make our way through the city tonight, so by daybreak, we are on the other side." Tanner pulled out a paper and opened it. "We need to find Ridge Street and follow it to Second Avenue. Go east on Second and it will take us to the end of the city."

They started down the pier, further looking for Ridge Street. After a few minutes, Lora pointed.

"There Ridge Street." They slowly picked their way up Ridge Street, passing more burning cans and homeless, who were trying to sleep as the rats ran around them. In this city, you never knew what kind of creatures you would see. All the races lived here and inter-mixed, and some odd-looking creatures came from that mix over the years. As they got farther into the city, the burning can were not around anymore and the homeless were far fewer. To either side of them, they could hear the taverns open and drunks yelling and singing.

"Just keep moving. This is the rough area. Once we get through here, it is smooth sailing," Tanner whispered to them. Tanner looked ahead of them again to see two half human, half dwarf standing in front of them.

"Well, well, what do we have here?" the one said to the other.

"Look, we are just passing through." Tanner held up his hands.

Three more appeared behind them. The two on each side.

"No trouble at all, just give us what we want," the first one who spoke said as they all started to close in on them.

Before Tanner could stop him, Rex grabbed the bow off his back. His wings opened, and he went to the air.

"You'll be sorry you messed with us," Rex yelled as he pulled and released.

The attackers all laughed.

"He has no arrows!" one yelled.

"What a moron," came from another.

He pulled and released several more times and still nothing. The attackers were still laughing and pointed yelling insults at him. One pulled out a slingshot and hit his right wing, breaking it. Rex yelled in pain as he crashed to the ground right by Tanner. As Rex tried to pull himself together, the attackers started to close in again. Rex and Lora grabbed their short swords. Tanner picked up the bow, and the magic exploded into him, up his arm and through his body, in seconds. He no longer had control; voices all seemed so distance. In seconds, he heard laughter, then screams, then silence, then everything went black.

Rex and Lora watched as Tanner grabbed the bow. They could tell something happened but never expected what happened next. In seconds, Tanner was in the air. The attackers laughed again.

"He has no arrows either." But Tanner pulled and released, and three lightning arrows hit the three coming from behind, and before those three hit the ground, he sent two more arrows at the two on the right. Those arrows didn't even hit them before he had two more on the way to the two at the front. The two on the left tried to run, but it was too late. In seconds, they all lay dead, and Tanner was out cold on the ground. Rex and Lora stood in disbelief.

"We need to go," Lora finally said.

Rex picked him up and put him over his right shoulder, grunting past the pain of his broken wing. Lora grabbed the bow and followed. A few streets later, they found Second Avenue and turned east on it. This street was nicer, and no one was sleeping on the ground here. They kept moving, but at a slower pace, and by daybreak, they were close to the end of the city.

* * * * *

The trio of dwarfs made it to the safe rest area, one of the many setups along the river path. The next morning, it was raining hard. The ate breakfast and set out.

"We can't afford to wait out the rain, so we will go slow. Sorry to say, it doesn't look like it's going to stop anytime soon." Nonmumi was pointing to the dark sky. It was dark as far as they could see. With that, they set out. "Stay close," Nonmumi said as they started.

There was no talking today. They had a hard time trying to maintain their footing as the path turned to mud and keeping the rain out of their faces. Shortly after lunch, they reached a point where the river went right.

"This is where we leave the river path. We will be safer following the forest path." He pointed to an overgrown path that no one really used anymore. He moved on without waiting for them to respond. They both sighed and followed.

The path was overgrown; they had to pull out short swords to try and cut their way through. The trees did, however, create an umbrella over them, so the rain didn't hit as hard and it wasn't as muddy here. There were a lot more stones this way and they were wet, so they were slipping unconsciously. By late afternoon, the rain seemed to get heavier, and it was getting harder to see where they were going and they had all fallen a couple of times. Nonmumi spied a group of pines they could get under easy enough and be shielded from the rain. He looked back at the other two and saw how tired they both looked and knew what lay ahead for them. They would need their strength. He pointed to the trees, and they all headed for them. They sat up against the trunk of the tree and shivered as they were all soaked to the bone and chilled. After a short time, the rain finally slowed down to a drizzle. They had eaten a little, but no one talked much as they were so tired.

Nonmumi held up his hand and pointed to his ear, wanting them to listen. They looked at each other confused. Then they heard a noise. At first they thought they were hearing things, but then it got louder and louder. Something or someone was crashing up the path and not trying to hide the fact that it was there. They got as close to the ground as they could. Whatever this was, it was big.

Nonmumi drew his battle ax. Dagrel drew his short sword; both moved in front of Arastrude. Then it came into view. A troll! Ten feet tall, hunched over, with long black hair falling to either side of his head. Skin a pale green, his big feet slamming the ground as he walked. He carried a small pack with him and wore torn-up shirt and pants. As he got closer, they could hear him muttering something. Then they realized he was crying. They all looked at one another, not sure what to do. So they sat and waited. The troll stopped fifty yards away and sat down.

"Where are my friends?" The troll sobbed. "The pretty lady said they would be here."

They tried harder to blend into the ground, and the troll continued to sit and sob.

Nonmumi whispered in Dagrel's ear, "Is your sword doing anything?"

Dagrel just shook his head no.

"Follow me." Nonmumi pointed at Arastrude to stay. They came out from the trees. He pointed for Dagrel to stay to the back of the troll. He came to the front.

"State your business, troll," Nonmumi demanded with his battle ax in hand.

The troll stopped crying and looked up.

"Friends, you are here." The troll got up and, in two steps, was on top of him.

"Hold up, troll!" Nonmumi backed up. "Why do you call me friend?" He was confused. Trolls were supposed to be mean and stupid. This one speaks and wants friends.

"Pretty lady said I'd find three friends here."

"What pretty lady?"

"Pretty lady that talked to me in my dreams."

Dagrel worked his way around the sword, but the sword did nothing. Not that he had any idea of what it might do, but it felt very calm. Arastrude came up behind him; they walked slowly toward Nonmumi.

"Who was the pretty lady?" Nonmumi asked.

"Don't know, she was nice. Told me I'm nice. That I'm right."

"Right about w—" He didn't get to finish because the troll saw the other two coming over.

"More friends, just like she said. Pretty lady smart."

"Do you have a name?" Arastrude asked softly.

"O."

"Your name is O?"

"Yes, that's me." He smiled from ear to ear.

"Nice to meet you, O. I'm Arastrude, and these are my friends Dagrel and Nonmumi."

"I so happy to have nice friends."

"What was the lady right about?" Nonmumi asked again, clearly annoyed that the other two came over.

"She said I was good and that I'm smart."

"Why are you good?" Dagrel asked.

"Because I don't want to hurt others. I'm nice."

"I see. What are you doing in this part of the lands?" Nonmumi asked.

"I was with a few other trolls. They are bad trolls."

"Why are they bad?" Nonmumi asked.

"They want to hurt pretty ladies' house."

They all looked at one another, knowing what that meant. They were on their way to the temple.

"Is her house by the waterfalls?" Arastrude asked.

"Yes, very pretty, bad to hurt it."

"Where are the other trolls now?" Nonmumi asked.

"They hurt humans. Don't know why."

The three of them realized things are much worse than they knew.

"Where are the bad trolls, O?" Arastrude pressed.

"Left them two days ago when pretty lady told me to come here."

"What did the pretty lady want you to do?" Dagrel asked.

"To find three friends and I found you."

"Then what?" Dagrel asked.

He seemed to think for a moment.

"I'm to help the one with the sword and protect the one with a stone."

"I see."

"What do my friends need me to do?"

"Can I just speak to my friends a minute alone?" Nonmumi said.

"OK." O smiled.

The three walked back by the trees that they were hiding in moments earlier.

"Clearly the goddess has sent him to warn us," Nonmumi said as the other two nodded in agreeance. "Did your sword get warm or do anything?"

"No, it felt oddly calm."

"That's a good sign. We need to get to the temple and the elves so they know what's going on. Trolls tend to move slowly, and they may look for him before moving on, but we also have to meet with the humans."

"How are we going to do that?" Arastrude asked.

"I think we are going to have to split up." He looked back at the troll who sat playing with his bag. "Do you think you can trust him?"

They both looked at each other.

"The goddess sent him for a reason," Dagrel finally said.

"I want him to go with you two to the falls to help the elves." They were quiet for a minute. "I can make better time on my own, get to Vwnrugh, send a word back to the council to send help to the falls. Then catch up with the humans, and then we will meet you at the falls."

"OK," they both agreed with him.

They all looked at one another, not sure if they were doing the right thing.

"My sword will keep us safe if he turns," Dagrel said.

"Be safe. Don't take your eyes off him. The goddess sent him sure enough, but he is still a troll," Nonmumi said.

With that, they walked back over to O.

"O, I need your help," Nonmumi said.

"OK, pretty lady told me to help."

"I have some things I have to do, so I can't get these two to the falls. Can you help get them there?"

O looked at them. He saw the sword and the bag with the stone.

"The sword and the stone, that's who I am supposed to help. Yes, I'll do it."

"I need you to protect them."

"I will, I will." O nodded his head yes several times.

They went about separating the items. Nonmumi got his things together, reminded O of his promise one more time, and was headed off west, wanting to get to the lake by nightfall. The new trio started south, wanting to make it to the lake as well.

CHAPTER 7

Scott left the next morning as well. He had taken a boat from Lorn to Moray. There had been talk of starting a trade route by boat, and he wanted to see if that would work. The waters were rough and damaged his boat. They had made the repairs at Moray and tried to strengthen the boat more, but the ride back was just as rough. Scott's thoughts were not on the trade route now though. What was he going to tell the city council? They would need to prepare and do it fast. How would he get everyone on board with him? Alastrine's name carried a lot of weight, and they would want to do what he asked of them. The evacuation of the city, he wasn't sure about though. He thought most would think they could stand against the trolls.

"Sir, we are coming into Lorn now, and none too soon. I'm afraid the boat has taken another beating and is going to require more repairs."

"Thank you. Start the repairs as soon as possible."

"Oh, and you have someone waiting for you." The man smiled and walked away. He could hear others on the boat snickering as well. He looked up to see Rosemary walking the docks, watching as they came closer. He just hung his head; he had hoped to not have to deal with her right away.

Rosemary was a large women who, when she walked on the pier, tested its strength. She had brown hair and eyes, and she believed she was a gift to the city. Her family was part of the founding fathers. It was a member of her family that served as the first governor of the city, and she never had a problem reminding people of that. There was a small group of ladies that followed her and acted like they were better than everyone. Rosemary's mother disapproved of how she acted, but that didn't seem to bother her.

As Scott got off the boat, she started.

"Governor, we need to talk." Rosemary sauntered toward him with an umbrella that didn't come near to covering her.

"I am sure we do, Rosemary, but I have other matters I need to tend to." Scott smiled at her.

"There are farmers showing up wanting shelter from trolls. Now I don't think we have room."

Scott cut her off.

"What are you talking about?"

A young boy ran down the deck.

"Sir, the council is waiting for you. There have been troll attacks on the farm. Some are coming here."

"Excuse me, boy, I was talking to the governor first." Rosemary was appalled at being interrupted.

"As I was saying, this city is very full as it is, and the buildup by the dock has already cluttered my view from my front porch. I won't tolerate anymore."

"Let's go, boy. We shouldn't keep the council waiting." Scott didn't respond to her and ran down the docks.

"We will continue this discussion later, Governor," she yelled to him as she stomped her foot. "What are you looking at?" she spat at one of the men on the boat, and she waddled off.

Scott walked into the town hall. It was a small building that was one big meeting room. There was a table across the front of the room where the council sat, and benches filled the rest of the room for the public to sit during the monthly meeting. An older man rose.

"Scott, thank the goddess you're back."

"Yes, Jess, I have heard what is going on, and what you are probably thinking is true." Scott reached his seat and sat down.

"Then the shadows are back." The old man turned pale.

"Yes, the chosen have been picked and are on their way to restore the balance."

"How much time do we have?" a young black man asked.

"Not much, Joseph."

Joseph was new to the council and was in charge of security for the city. He was a large man, six foot three, had black wavy hair and brown eyes. His smile melted hearts but don't cross him.

"Then I have much work to do." He stood to leave.

"Just a minute, we need to tell Scott of the vote." Jess stopped him.

"What vote?" Scott was confused.

"We voted that if the shadows were back that you have absolute authority. Decisions will have to be made that can't wait for a vote. We have great confidence in you. Take care of our city." Scott was shocked and had no idea what to say as the board dismissed itself. They all walked out except Joseph.

"I am here to do whatever it is you need. The others are older and don't have the energy anymore." Joseph put his hand on Scott's shoulder

"Thanks, you. You are a good friend, and I will need all the help I can get. You work on defending the city. I have other things to start working on. I will check in with you later." Scott looked up at the big man and saw uncertainty in his eyes. "We will get thought this."

They both got up and headed out of the hall.

* * * * *

Felix, Leigh, and Whiley started down through the fields and soon saw farmers heading toward Lorn. They were carrying with them what they could. They decided it would be best if they kept out of sight. So they moved from trees to shrubs and rocks that were scattered around, anything they could hide in and look for the next place to jump to and make sure they were not seen. They did run into a farmer and his kids once. They warned them about the trolls coming and how they were ripping humans apart. Whiley thanked them and moved on.

"Felix, it is getting late. We need to find shelter," Leigh finally said. They were all exhausted from the stress of trying to stay safe.

"We need to get to the river. We will be safer by the water," Felix rebutted

"It's getting dark. Clouds are moving in. A storm may be coming." Leigh pointed to the south where the dark clouds were moving in.

Felix looked and sighed. He looked at Whiley who was so drained he didn't offer any thing to the conversation.

"Whiley, what do you think?" Felix asked to the shock of Whiley and Leigh.

"What do I think? I think my head is about to split in half. I'm trying to understand what it is that I am to do. I'm trying to remember the history but can't. I'm trying to hide from trolls and whatever else may be after us. What do I think? I think this is all crazy, and I want it to end. That's what I think." Whiley was almost yelling by the time he was done and had tears in his eyes. Leigh grabbed him and hugged him tightly.

"OK, we find a place to rest for the night and eat something. Leigh will explain things to you," Felix said as he looked around for somewhere to rest.

"Leigh, you mean you know the whole story?" He took a step back and looked at him shocked.

"Yes, Alastrine told me to talk to you, but we have been moving and I haven't had time."

Whiley smiled, relief shown on his face. He hugged Leigh hard.

"Are you OK?" Leigh asked as he stumbled back.

"Yes, you have answers I need."

"OK, boys, we need to move. There is nothing here that works. We have to keep looking. That storm is coming."

They started looking, and after about half an hour, they found a farmhouse that was abandoned with a small pond close by.

"This will do," Felix said. "We can stay in the farmhouse. If trouble comes, there is the water from the pond to help. You two go in and see if there is any food left behind. I'm going to bless the pond just in case we need it."

Leigh entered the farmhouse, sword drawn, with Whiley close behind. It was a small one-bedroom house—living room, kitchen, bedroom was all. They had left recently and had done so in a hurry. Once they felt safe, they looked to see what was in the kitchen. There wasn't much. Some dried meats and fresh fruit was all, but that saved on their own supplies so they ate that. Felix joined them as they sat the chairs upright and ate at a small table. They ate in silence as they were all exhausted. After they ate, Leigh and Whiley went into the bedroom to see what was there to sleep on. Just a wooden frame. The bed pad was gone. They went back into the living room. There was two small couches, so they each took one. They tried to get comfortable but couldn't really stretch out on them. Felix had said to get what sleep they could. He was going to watch from the front porch for any trouble. Felix sat on a wood beam that held the roof of the porch so as not to be seen.

"So what can you tell me?" Whiley asked after a few minutes of lying there.

"You are the wielder and I am the protector," Leigh responded after a few minutes.

"The what?" Whiley propped himself up on an elbow.

"You don't know your history very well, do you?"

"Not much use for it on the streets. I do remember something about shadows."

Leigh explained the history to him and what was now happening. Whiley sat up and listened without interrupting.

"So the goddess chose me? Why?" he asked after Leigh had finished talking.

"Don't know. She doesn't give reasons, don't have to."

"So I use the stone in this bag to help heal the lands?"

"Yes, along with the other three. You send the energy through a crystal, and it will bring balance back to the lands and get rid of the shadows."

Whiley sat up and opened the bag. Felix flew in as Leigh jumped up.

"Don't touch it!" Leigh yelled.

"It's old magic," Felix yelled.

"OK, sorry, guys, just wanted to see what it is I am supposed to use." Whiley held his hands up.

"You will when we get to the elves, and they can help you with the magic," Felix said.

Whiley lowered the flap and patted it against the bag. The stone reacted to his touch and sent magic flying into him. He felt his right hand and arm surge with the power of the magic and then it overtook his body. His eyes got wide, then rolled up into his head and everything went black.

"What happened?" Leigh yelled as he got to him just before he hit the floor.

"It reacted to his touch even through the bag."

"What do we do?"

"This is bad." Felix shook his head.

"I know we don't have a lot of time. How long do you think he will be out?"

"Don't know, but even worse, any shadows in the area will have noticed the magic being used."

They looked at each other, a little panic was setting in. Leigh got him on the couch and made sure he was still breathing. Leigh took a deep breath and sat down.

"Alastrine was right," Felix said to him.

"Right about what?"

"You do have feelings for him." Felix smiled

"I'm worried is all."

"I saw your face when he went down. That was more than worry."

"What is your point?"

"The goddess chose well is all."

"What does that mean?"

"It mean you would give your life for him, and that is what a protector is supposed to do."

"Do you think he knows?" Leigh looked at him, smiling.

"Time will tell. Now try and get some rest."

CHAPTER 8

Luvon and Elyon met the king the next morning. Ayre was waiting for them in the garden again. The morning was cool, but the sun coming up in the clear sky promised a nice day. They bowed as they came to the king, and he returned in kind.

"I trust you only told whom you had to?"

"Yes, Your Majesty," they both said.

"I want to thank you again on behalf of the elves for the sacrifice you are making." He put a hand on each of their shoulders.

"Thank you, Your Majesty," the both said again.

"Time is short. We must head to the pier. Captain Folmar and the boats are waiting to take you to the temple," Ayre said as he lead them out of the garden. "There are three boats. You will be in the middle boat. The other two boats will have bowmen to protect you," he explained as they walked.

They walked in silence through the quiet streets of Lyloth. It was early yet, and most were still asleep or just waking up. They each got lost in their own thoughts.

Ayre was thinking about all the mornings he spent in his gardens. Time spent thinking and solving problems that now seemed silly. He wished for the silliness again. He looked at the streets of his city and wondered how much longer they would be safe. What form of trouble would the shadows bring? They had almost killed off the four races last time. What would happen this time? Were the other races prepared? He was sure. Alastrine would do his best, but would they listen?

Luvon was thinking about fishing with his friends. The sunny afternoons they spent by the water. They never really caught any fish;

half the time they just ended up in the water or just sat laughing and telling jokes. He wondered if he would ever hear their laughs again. He wished he was able to tell them the truth about where he was going. He had told them the king asked him to go on a hunting trip, that the deer were overrunning parts of the forest and needed to be thinned out. They all told him how lucky he was. He really didn't feel lucky.

Elyon's thoughts went to her grandmother. She spent a lot of time with her. The stories her grandmother told always made her smile even if she had already heard them a thousand times. She would cook with her, but she really liked baking with her; she was the one who had started the bakery and handed it down to her mother. She would always tell her, someday, it will be hers. She wanted to bake with her again. She had told her mother the truth but told her grandmother that the king asked her help with baking at the palace. The baker there wasn't feeling well, so she may be gone awhile. Her grandmother was so excited for her. She smiled and felt bad for lying to her but didn't want her worrying.

"Your Majesty, good to see you. Luvon, Elyon, we are ready for you," Captain Folmar said as they got to the pier, bringing them all back from their thoughts.

Captain Folmar was an older elf who had been serving for many years. He had blond hair pulled back into a ponytail and blue eyes and was well versed with the bow and short sword. There were three boats like the king had said there would be. They were small boats only holding two to three elves; they were built for speed, very narrow to cut through the water fast. There were three bowmen in the front one and in the back one. The middle one sat empty.

"Captain Folmar, thank you for getting ready so fast," Ayre said as he returned his bow.

"Anything for you, Your Majesty. Always ready to serve." Folmar smiled back.

"Make sure these two arrive safe at the temple." Ayre turned to Luvon and Elyon. "Again, I thank you. Yours is a great responsibility. I have great faith that you will do fine. I must go now. I have other matter to deal with." Ayre shook both of their hands and helped Elyon into the boat.

"No worries, Your Majesty. They are in good hands." Folmar smiled as he pushed off.

Ayre turned and went back up the path he had just come done. They were already starting down the river. The ride to the end of the forest would take most of the day. Then there was the plateau that was totally bare of plants. It ran and dropped off to the valley below. They would have to leave the boats and walk to the stairs that were carved into the side of the cliffs. They led down to the temple at the bottom. The temple sat beside the waterfalls and was cut into the cliffs.

They floated along at a good pace. The current was strong and took them out of the city fast. Now all they saw was trees and, from time to time, a house. The ride was nice and easy, and they relax.

* * * * *

Roger went to Perth and had to make his way through people who were fleeing their homes in fear of the trolls. He started hearing more of the same stories he had heard earlier in the day. More tears and sorrow than he had seen in his whole life. He couldn't believe how fast things were happening. He was sure not even Alastrine was ready for this already. He made it into the city where things were a mass confusion. Some shops had closed and boarded up already. Others were being overrun with people looking for supplies.

"Roger, thank the goddess you're back." A young man ran up to him.

"Patrick, what is going on?" Roger asked as he got off his horse.

Patrick was a member of the council. There were five members representing the five sections of the city. Patrick was older than Roger but not by much. He had olive skin and black hair and brown eyes.

"Everyone is in panic. The stories of the trolls and you at a meeting with Alastrine, people fear that the shadows are back." Patrick looked into Roger's eyes, and Roger said nothing.

"They are right, aren't they?"

"Where is the rest of council?" Roger asked.

"At city hall waiting for you. We got word you were back, so I came to find you."

"Then to city hall we go."

Patrick and Roger made their way down the crowded street to city hall. It was a small building with a large meeting room downstairs and Roger's office and a smaller meeting room upstairs. The council was waiting for him in the smaller meeting room.

"Roger, what news do you have?" One of the members stood as he walked in.

Roger was not really prepared for that question. He was still putting it all together himself.

"The balance has shifted," he said after a few minutes of all of them staring at him.

There was silence as they all took in what that meant.

"Many in the city have already come to that conclusion," one of the members said softly.

"Our city sits in a bad location. We can be circled and trapped here," another member said.

"Some have already packed up and are going to Lorn," Patrick said.

"We can defend this city," Roger said, not believing how defeated they all sounded.

"Roger, we understand your love of this city, but—," one of the members started.

"But nothing. We can't just give up," Roger interrupted.

"We are not giving up. We just think that our resources would be better used in Lorn," another member said.

"Wait, what are you saying?" Roger was confused.

"We voted while you were gone, when the stories started coming in."

"Voted on what?"

"That if the balance had shifted, we would shut the city down and help Lorn. That was our best bet to survive," Patrick said.

Roger had tears in his eyes. He could not believe that he was supposed to leave his city hall without a fight.

"They could easily trap us here. What would we do? No help would come," another board member said.

"My family started this city I can't let it die." Roger was choked up now.

"It will die either way. If we go to Lorn, we may have a chance to come back and rebuild. If we stay, we become part of the rubble," Patrick said.

"Motion to carry out the vote of closing the city?" one member asked.

"I," came from another member.

"Second."

"I," came from another member.

"All in favor."

"I," came from all five members.

"Opposed."

"The Is have it. When I close this meeting, this council is no more and the city of Perth will be evacuated." Patrick picked the gavel.

"Patrick, don't do it," Roger begged.

"I'm sorry, my friend." With that, Patrick pounded the gavel and ended Perth as a city.

Roger sat down on a chair and began to cry. The member got up and left in silence.

CHAPTER 9

Lor paced back and forth in his den. He had been thinking ever since the meeting the night before and was concerned that the council might try and get rid of him. He stopped walking from time to time as an idea came to him, and then he shut it down as fast as it came, and he would start walking again.

"Sir, if I may?" Curr said. He was young with a black beck, brown hair and eyes. He acted like everyone loved him although he knew better but never let that show. He was the one Lor called upon when he was in a jam. He had met him in Juna once when he found himself in a spot that he needed help with. Since then, Lor had called on him many times for many things. He was probably the most untrusted man in Coll, certainly one of the most disliked. Rumor had it that he was the one who murdered Mir, but that was hard to prove. Lor would never push the issue, saying he wanted his father to rest in peace. Many didn't buy that at all and believed that Lor had Curr kill Mir.

"No, you may not. I need to think. When I am ready for you, I will let you know."

"Yes, well, your thoughts have gotten you very far." Curr smirked.

"I have done very well on my own, thank you," Lor spat back.

"So you don't want my help?"

"No, I don't need your kind of help right now."

"Are you sure?" He was sitting at Lor's desk with his dagger pointing at the desk, spinning it as he talked.

"Put that away. I need to do something to put me back in favor with the public." Curr laughed.

"They never liked you, but at least they used to hide that fact. Then you questioned the goddess in public. Stupid move. Now they have no problem showing how much they hate you." Curr laughed again.

"This can be fixed." Lor slammed his hand on the desk. "And you will help me once I figure out what to do."

"Don't you think you should be more concerned with the shadows and trolls?" Curr slammed his hand on the desk to show he didn't fear Lor.

"My son will fix that problem." He waved Curr off.

"Your son!" He laughed out loud. "You must be kidding."

"It was a mistake that he was not the chosen one. He will prove that when he has to handle the magic because it is too strong for the others."

"OK, you do understand he is not the chosen one, and the magic will not work for him," Curr almost yelled at him now.

"If you are not going to offer any help, you can leave." Lor turned his back and walked away.

"You need me, Lor. I don't need you. Let's get that straight. So I would be careful turning your back to me so quickly," Curr spat at him, now feeling his anger rise.

"I don't need anyone. I can use you as I have in the past, or I can get others if you can't do what I need." Lor didn't look back at him.

"You live in a fantasy world. Who do you think would take time to help you besides me? You may have passed me as the most hated man in the city."

"I told you that can be fixed." Lor spun to face him now.

"You don't intimidate me, Lor. I know who you are. You are just like me, only you hide behind a fake personality. The problem is that everyone is seeing through it now."

"I am nothing like you," Lor replied, anger now flowing from him.

"Really? When the rest of the council is out getting ready for what is to come, where are you? You are here worrying about who likes you. Face it, all you care about is you. Just like me, only I am fine with admitting it."

"I care for this city with everything I have!"

"You believe your own lies," Curr cut him off.

"Get out. I don't need you." Lor pointed to the door and looked away from him.

"Fine, but I am right and you know it. That is why you are angry." Curr picked up his dagger and headed toward the door. "You'll come looking for me again. You always do when you need someone to do your dirty work." Curr slammed the door to the den as he left.

Lor watched out the window as Curr walked down the street.

"Another problem I need to deal with," he said out loud.

* * * * *

Alastrine went back to his house, lit a white and blue candle, sat on the floor in front of them, and began to meditate. He soon found himself sitting in his safe place—under a large apple tree on a small hilltop surrounded by wild flowers. He breathed in the fresh air. How he loved his safe place. Then a bright light appeared before him. The reason he was here. It was the goddess. He came to talk to her often when things were troubling him.

"My son, what is it you need of me?" Her beautiful voice sang in his head.

"Things seem to be moving faster than I thought, my lady."

"Yes, I see this. You need to adjust your plans."

"I worry my plans won't work. What if it is too little too late?"

"Trust yourself, my son. I do."

"The future of the four races is riding on decisions I make."

"That is a lot for one to handle, but you are good under pressure. You know what you need to do."

"I will do everything I can, my lady."

"Remember, you are not alone. Others are doing things as well. The chosen are out there doing what they need to do."

"Yes, my lady."

"I have great faith in all I have chosen. It will be a long path, but you will make it."

"Thank you, my lady."

"Have faith, my son." And with that, the goddess was gone and he was back sitting on the floor of his houses.

"Bless be, my lady," Alastrine said as he put out the candles, packed what he needed, and headed back out.

As Alastrine came to the gate, Alex was there waiting for him.

"People are still coming in," Alex said, stress showing on his face. "Thankfully, most now are coming for safety and have not seen any trolls."

"So the troll sightings are near the mountains? That's good."

"Seems that way."

"That's a break we needed. Now do you have what I asked for?"

"Yes, they are by the gate waiting, and there is a horse ready for you."

"Good. Don't delay on what I asked you to do. Time is short. I can't stress that enough. We can't waste time," Alastrine said as they walked over to where the men were waiting.

"Men, most of you know this is Alastrine. He is the keeper and has asked you to help him."

"Things are not good. It's going to be a fight, but we must slow the trolls to let the city reinforce itself if it is to have a chance to survive," Alastrine said to all of them.

They all nodded as they had already been informed by Alex.

"These three boys are your messengers—Joel, Shawn, and Parker."

"Boys." He looked at the three who were probably just past their sixteenth summer.

"What you will be doing is very important. You must deliver the messages exactly as I tell you. Can you do that?"

"Yes, sir," they all replied.

"These three men are the creative ones," Alex said as he moved to the next three in line. "This is Tony, Lance, and Brian."

"Men, we have to come up with creative ways to slow down these trolls. Can you do it?"

"It's all in our bags, sir," Tony said as he patted the saddlebag.

"And these are the nine bowmen you wanted." Alex moved to the next in line. "This is Ron, Lucky, Hank, Lapper, Will, Ted, Mel, Nick, and AJ."

"Men, you have a tough job of hit and run. We can't fight them toe to toe. They would crush us. So we have to hit and be gone fast before the arrows reach their targets."

They all nodded that they understood.

"Then we should be off. We ride most of the way but will have to go on foot at some point." Alastrine looked at Alex. "Remember to do as I ask. It is important so we can save as many lives as we can." Alastrine mounted his horse and rode out of the gate with the rest in tow.

Alex watched for a few moments till he couldn't see them. He turned and headed back to the meeting hall. He had asked for several men to meet him there to help him accomplish what Alastrine had asked him to do. He wondered as he walked if he would ever see again any of the men that just left. He took a deep breath and walked on. Tears filled his eyes as he was still trying to cope with what was coming.

CHAPTER 10

Scott left his house early the next morning. He had planned on meeting with several men who would help lead the defense and escape of the city. He did not sleep well; he did not agree with the council giving him and only him the power to make decisions. That was a weight he wasn't sure he was ready for. If he made a misstep and lots of lives were lost, he didn't know how he would deal with that.

"Governor," came a shrill voice from behind him. He stopped, knowing, without looking, who it was and couldn't believe that she was even up this time of day.

"Rosemary, how lovely to see you," he responded as he turned to meet her.

"I know it is. You know what's not lovely to see?"

"No, but I'm sure you are going to tell me."

"All these poor people coming into the city. I mean, we really don't have the room."

"Well, we all have to make sacrifices in time like this." Scott half smiled.

"I don't, and another thing, don't you think these poor will attract the trolls?"

"I don't think they care if you're rich or poor. Listen, I—"

"Now you listen. These poor better not bring trolls or you will have some answering to do." She flicked a paper fan in front of her face and turned and walked away.

"She is a handful, isn't she?" Joseph said, standing behind Scott and scaring him.

"I didn't hear you come up. She has some nerve. I want to tell her about herself just once. Just once." Scott took a deep breath and looked up at Joseph.

"I have started to work on the wall and some traps in front to slow them down."

"That's good. Time is short. Follow me. I have to go to the docks."

The two men walked down to the dock where an old man sat, waiting for them.

"Noah, my friend, are the warehouses ready?" Scott shook the old man's hand as he talked.

"Yes, sir, they are." He smiled.

"What are you doing with the warehouses?" Joseph asked.

"Noah is going to start storing food and getting it ready to distribute if or when we have to flee the city."

"You don't have faith in me?" Joseph looked hurt.

"No, that's not it at all, but I don't think we can stand alone against the trolls and I don't think the elves, dwarfs, or hawk people are going to get here in time even if they wanted to, which I don't think they want to anyway. I'm sure they blame us for the balance shifting."

"You really think that?" Joseph was surprised.

"I do, but we got more to do." They headed to the south gate.

"Ahh, sir, we are ready to go," a young man said as they came to the gate.

"Now you understand what I need you to do?" Scott asked.

"Yes, sir, we are to go to all the farmers' field close by and get anything that is ready and bring it back to the warehouses." The young man smiled.

"You have to be back by dusk. I don't want anyone out at night. It is too risky."

"Yes, sir, we have three parties of twenty-one in each. They all know what to do."

"Then be off. Report to me when all parties are back."

"Yes, sir." The young man went off through the gate.

"It seems like you are getting it all together," Joseph said.

"I'm trying. My wife is working with those that are coming in. She has started a tent city outside the east gate."

"What till Rosemary hears that." Joseph half laughed.

"Yeah, thanks," he sighed.

"Well, good news. I have Dylan in charge of training men with bows and swords."

"That was a good choice. Keep working on what you're doing and report back to me this evening."

"No problem. We will make it. It will be OK." He patted Scott on the back.

"I'm going to go check on my wife. I hope you're right." They shook hands and parted.

* * * * *

Tanner fluttered his eyes, not sure what had happened. Once his vision cleared a bit, he realized he was flying. The sky around him was the bluest sky he had ever seen. There was a warm breeze ruffling his feathers. It almost tickled him, but he loved it. There was not a cloud to be seen. He thought for a minute and got scared. Had the magic killed him? Was this the summer lands? Was this where you go when you die? Then he looked around some more and realized he was in his safe place. The place he would go when he meditated. But how did he get here this time?

"You are not dead," a soft gentle voice answered his question. "I brought you here to talk to you."

He thought to ask who are you.

"Do you not know who I am?"

"My lady." He realized with a smile.

"Yes, I am Goddess Atla. I have chosen you, Tanner, to be a protector. You are a good soul, an old soul, who has been loyal to me."

"Thank you, my lady. I am loyal because you are good and protect us," Tanner said, smiling. He loved feeling her around him; it always felt so peaceful.

He smiled as he flew, knowing that the breeze in his face and the blue sky, it all was the goddess; and she surrounded him everywhere. He loved it here.

"Yes, Tanner, this is your summer land, or what you believed it to be," the soft voice came again.

He smiled. He didn't ever want to leave here. He didn't think he had ever been so happy. Then another thought crossed his mind. His friends, were they OK? He had forgotten about them. He was supposed to protect them.

"They are fine. Rex is carrying you and Lora is following. They are almost out of the city."

"I love it here. I don't want to go," he said, smiling broadly.

"I have placed great trust in you, and your people need you."

"Why me?"

"Because I have chosen you. I know you can handle the responsibility. You are very strong."

Tanner looked out across the sky; it was turning black in the distance and seemed to be coming toward him.

"What it that?" Tanner asked, looking at its coming.

"It is the reason I picked the chosen ones."

"The shadows." A knot formed in his stomach.

"It is coming and wants to end life as you know it."

Tears came to his eyes. He knew what he had to do.

"Remember, Tanner, the magic is strong. You can't control it, and don't let is control you." Tanner looked confused.

"I know you don't understand. It's not easy. You have to be one with the magic. It is in your system now and will always be. It will try to control you. Don't let it. Try and control it, and it won't work for you. Work in harmony as nature does, and the outcome will be what you want."

"How do I do that?"

"You will learn."

He went to ask another question but felt sleepy all of a sudden.

"Time to go back and do as I have asked you, dear Tanner. You will do fine. When you wake, you will be with your friends again."

He was out before he could protest.

CHAPTER 11

Alfozmit entered a private room in his home, looked out the door one more time to make sure no one was around, then closed the door. The only light came from under the door. But he knew his way around the room. He had been in here several times during the election to ask for help. Now he was back to pay up, and he wasn't sure he wanted to do this. He moved to the altar and lit a match and held it by the black candle that he had used to ask for help many times before. He reached over slowly and lit the candle.

"My lady, are you here?" he asked slowly.

"Yes, my son. I was starting to think you weren't going to pay up," her voice came soft into his head.

"Never, my lady. I am thankful for your help," he lied.

"You know you would have never became governor of Vwnrush without my help," her voice came again.

"I am thankful, my lady."

"You should be," her voice, now a little louder, came to him.

"I will honor you in every way, my lady."

"You will do more than that," her voice came again, sounding evil now.

"What do you want, my lady?"

"You need to pledge your allegiance to me."

"What, my lady?"

"That was the deal. You said you would do as I wished. That is what I wish."

"What does that mean?" He was now nervous.

"It doesn't matter what it means." She laughed.

"What if I refuse?" he asked, not sure if he wanted to know the answer.

"You don't want to cross me, mortal!" she yelled in his head.

"No, I would never, my lady."

"Then pledge your allegiance to me."

He hesitated for a moment.

"Now!"

"I pledge my allegiance to you, my lady, Goddess Hel."

"Thank you." She laughed.

He started feeling funny.

"What's happening to me?"

"One of my shadows is taking over."

"You're killing me."

"No, just taking over. You will still be there, seeing and hearing everything. You just have no control." She laughed in his head.

"No, stop! I don't want this."

"It's too late."

His spirit was pushed deep down inside of himself; he felt trapped, and what was left of him would not be seen again, and he began to cry.

"Now you have to stop the humans that are coming this way."

"Yes, my lady," the shadow that now took over Alfozmit's body answered.

"They have one of the stones. We must stop them. It will be a boy and a girl. The girl will have the stone."

"What of the other stones?"

"Not to worry. I have surprises in store for all of them. We only need to stop one for them to fail. Then I will destroy all four races and my sister."

"Yes, my lady."

"First, you need to get the police force to swear their allegiance to you. That will allow shadows to take them over. Hire more. I want an army. The races will come here for a last stand, and I want to be ready for that."

"Yes, my lady."

"Nonmumi, a dwarf, is supposed to be meeting up with the humans here. Nonmumi is trouble. We need to take care of that. Put a warrant out for his arrest. Accuse him of being a traitor. Say he turned over the chosen to a troll."

"Yes, my lady."

"Now be off with you."

Alfozmit put out the candle and went off to do as he was told.

* * * * *

Luvon, Elyon, and company had made a good time on the river. Luvon had been shifting around in the boat for the last ten minutes or so and kept looking over his shoulder.

Folmar looked at the sun and realized it was around lunchtime.

"Pull to the shore over there, men." He pointed to a grassy area where they could get in and out of the boats easily.

"Why are we stopping?" Luvon asked.

"I can see you are getting hungry and cramped in the boat." Folmar smiled. "We won't be long here, and we will be on our way again."

They helped pull their boat ashore and get food out, but Luvon kept looking over his shoulder.

"What is wrong with you?" Elyon asked.

"Something is wrong. Don't you feel it?"

"Feel what?" Elyon was confused.

"It's like a vibration in the air. It is making me very uneasy."

"I don't feel anything." Elyon shrugged her shoulders.

"I think something is wrong."

They sat and ate quietly, and the others talked to one another, but none talked to them. Folmar came over at one point.

"Are you two doing OK?"

"Yes, we are, thank you," Elyon answered.

"Are we leaving soon?" Luvon asked.

"Shortly."

"Sir!" one of the men yelled and pointed to the boats.

They all turned to see three huge snakes wrapping themselves around the boats and squeezing them.

"They are smashing the boat! Men, fire at will!" Folmar yelled.

Arrows flew from several directions, hitting all three targets, but this did not deter them.

"Sir, have them bless their arrows and fire into the water," Elyon offered.

"Good idea. Men, bless your arrows and fire into the water," Folmar barked.

The men did, and the snakes hissed as the blessed water hit them.

"Shadows have taken them over," Luvon said.

"This close to the city. I don't believe it." Folmar was beside himself.

Luvon pulled the bow from his back, and the magic exploded into him, ripping through his body so hard and fast it took him by surprise. He pulled and released so fast he didn't even realize he did it, and in seconds, the snakes were dead. They all looked for a moment. Then one of the bowman yelled, "Look out!"

The bowman threw himself onto the side of a large wolf that had appeared out of nowhere and was almost on top of Elyon.

Folmar turned and went after the wolf with his short sword, driving it into the wolf's chest. It didn't seem to faze him at all. The wolf came back with a massive paw and sent him flying to the ground. The bowman who threw himself at the wolf was now trying to get out of the way but got kicked by the wolf's back legs, sending him tumbling onto a tree. Arrows flew over Luvon's and Elyon's heads and hit their target, but again, this didn't seem to faze him.

"Luvon, the shadows have this wolf," Elyon pointed out to him.

Luvon turned his bow on the wolf and had several shots off in seconds as the magic again raced through his body. He wasn't sure how much more of this he could take. The wolf was getting ready to attack again as Luvon's arrows hit him. There was a loud scream as the shadow died and slipped into the ground, and the wolf lay dead on the ground.

"The shadows know who we are. They won't stop, will they?" Elyon was getting a little overwhelmed.

"They will keep trying, I am sorry to say, my dear," Folmar said as he gathered himself.

"That is why we need to get you to the temple as soon as possible. We have to restore balance."

"Sir, the boats are all damaged," one of the bowmen said as he walked over to the boats.

"Can they be fixed." Folmar was trying to right himself but was obviously hurt.

"It will take several hours but yes."

"Then get started. Time is something we don't have a lot of."

The bowman who had thrown himself at the wolf was just starting to move, and it was plain to see he was hurt as well.

"The shadows are getting bold, coming this close to the elf city," Folmar mused.

"We should let the king know," Elyon said as she helped Luvon sit down. The magic had taken a lot out of him. He looked like he could pass out.

"That's a good idea, Elyon. Hang in there, Luvon. Let's move him close to the water and bless the water to protect us as much as we can while they fix the boat."

The two of them moved Luvon closer to the water and Elyon blessed it, then they sat and waited for the boats to get fix.

"We will send one boat back with two bowmen to warn the king. The rest of us will go on," Folmar had told everyone as they worked.

CHAPTER 12

The rain had stopped, and the sun came out as it was setting. There were just starting to dry out as Dagrel lead Arastrude and O. They were at the edge of the Hia Darum Forest. They could see Lomerick Lake off in the distance, but it was getting late.

"I think we should make camp here. We won't make it to the lake by dark, and it's too open to make camp on the plains," Dagrel said, looking for a spot that looked safe.

"I protect you," O said.

"Yes, of course, but we need to rest in a safe place," Arastrude said, patting his hand. O smiled at her. O had not left her side since the three of them had set out. Dagrel had taken the lead, looking to make sure they were safe.

"There." Dagrel pointed to a group of small boulders where some pine trees had grown close by. "That will be perfect." They moved there and sat and ate. They didn't build a fire. They didn't want to take a chance and be noticed.

"It is early, so why don't you and O sit and watch and I will sleep for a couple of hours?" Dagrel said to Arastrude.

"OK. O, you OK with that?" She smiled at him.

"O OK." He returned her smile.

"Remember, only let me sleep a couple of hours. Then you two can sleep."

"Yes, Dagrel a couple of hours. Now get some sleep."

Dagrel wasn't sure about the troll yet, but Arastrude had warmed right up to him. He wasn't sure if he liked that. He didn't know why it bothered him, but it did. The goddess had sent him; they felt sure about that. But as he lay there watching the two of them talk, he was annoyed. He rolled over. A couple hours would go fast and he needed sleep.

"O, do you have family?" Arastrude asked as they sat down. The darkness had already started creeping in around them, but she could still see his face. He was thinking, not sure what to say.

"Like a mother and father?" she finally said after a few moments.

"O only have pack." He held his small backpack.

"What's in the pack?"

"Given to me when I was young. All I have. Mom, Dad gone."

She felt sad for him as she rubbed his arm. Then a noise caught her attention. She looked back, and it was just Dagrel rolling over.

"Would you like to see what is in my pack?" O was excited.

"Yes, very much."

"O was told that long time ago and many fathers ago, the humans gave us this." O fumbled, opening the pack, and finally pulled out a clear bag with a little human who had blond hair and carried a blue stick. The bag was sucked in tight all around him.

"What is it?" Arastrude looked at it confused.

"O not know. Other trolls say junk from the old humans, but it's all O has." He put it back and pulled out another clear bag. It had an odd-looking cart with four black wheels. The bag was sucked in all around it as well. "This one says hot wheels on this side." He pointed to the bottom. "They don't feel hot to me though."

"What are the sacks they are in? I've never seen clear sacks that suck to things like that. Can you open it?"

"Must never open. O opened one and the golden book went away." He put that bag back and pulled out another one. "This is O's favorite."

She looked at it for a moment. "Green eggs and ham. Cat in the hat. What is that?" She was very confused.

"O not know. O ate green eggs once and got sick." He put it away and closed his bag.

"This is O's family. Used to be a lot more but bags got open and things go away, but this is all O has."

She thought how sad, but he seemed happy. She smiled at him as he held his pack, and they sat there quietly.

A few moments later, a loud thud scared both of them. They looked into the darkness to see what the noise was, and there stood three trolls.

* * * * *

Sherry stopped Alex as he headed toward a meeting.

"Alex, honey, we have problems," Sherry said. She was clearly exhausted.

"Honey, you need to get some rest." He hugged her. "Are the girls OK?" They had two girls: Sara, who was just past her seventeenth summer, and Bell, who was just past her eighth summer.

"Yes, they just showed up to help at the warehouses." She smiled. She was very proud of her girls; they were always ready to help out when needed. She knew she could always count on them.

"Walk with me, dear." He started moving again. "I have a meeting and lots to do."

"I know. Not to add to it, but we are running out of room and provisions, and people just keep coming. What do we do?"

He stopped and looked at her. Tears were in her eyes, and it tore him apart. He was getting tired himself, so he took a deep breath and ran ideas through his head fast. He looked around. There was a young boy walking by.

"Son, come here!" Alex yelled.

The boy stopped and looked.

"Yes, you come here."

"Yes, sir," the boy said as he approached.

"You are Tom's boy?"

"Yes, sir."

"Do me a favor. I need you to go to the meeting hall and tell the men waiting for me to bring the maps and come meet me at the warehouse."

"Yes, sir." The boy was off.

"OK, dear, to the docks." They headed off as Sherry was still trying to control her tears. They walked fast and passed more groups of farmers on their way to the warehouses. They got there and there was a line out the door. They pushed their way through; once inside,

Alex couldn't believe his eyes. The warehouse was packed elbow to elbow. Kids crying, a couple of ladies yelling and trying to get people in line to get food, people sleeping and standing up. The smell of sweat was overwhelming. He looked at the line for food, and there wasn't much there to eat.

"Is there no more food?" He looked at Sherry.

"Very little. The good news is that the people coming in now have some that they are sharing, but it won't last."

"Is the other warehouse the same?"

"Yes," she sighed heavily. "These people deserve better."

"Yes, dear, they do." He looked around more. "If something happens, we will never get all these people out in time." He shook his head.

"What can we do?"

"We have to move them now. Get them to Vwnrush."

"What if I got some ladies together and we made tents for people to stay in?"

"That's a great idea. Make them big enough for twenty or so. When you have four done, we will send the first group on their way. Then keep working like that. Send women and children first. We need the men here to help."

"OK, dear."

"Start getting the groups together so they are ready to go. I want them on the road as soon as possible. I'm going to send a message to Perth and Lorn to let them know what I am doing. They must be as crazy as we are."

She looked at him and didn't need to say a word; he could see it in her eyes. He took her by the shoulders and held her.

"Things are bad and going to get worse. I love you very much, and I need your help. Get this started for me so we can save as many lives as we can. Then get some rest when you can."

She nodded her head that she understood.

"OK, honey, the guys I need to meet with are coming. Are you OK?"

"Yes, dear." She paused, then looked back into his eyes. "Will we ever get back to the way it was?" He didn't answer, just hugged her and went back out the door. She felt her heart break a little inside.

CHAPTER 13

Roger was out walking in his city the next day. People were busy packing up and loading wagons. He talked to several who said they were sad to lose their city but understood why it had to be done. He tried to smile and reassure them that everything would be OK, but even he didn't believe that. He walked down by the river where boats were being loaded with lumber and other supplies to send to Lorn. *Supplies that should be used here*, he thought to himself.

"Roger, wait up," a voice came from behind him.

He turned to see Patrick coming toward him. He really didn't want to see him.

"What is it?" Roger asked as he caught up to him.

"I am worried about you."

"Really?" Roger said sarcastically and started walking again.

"You know we did the right thing!" Patrick yelled at him as he walked away.

"Do I? How do you know what I am thinking?" Roger spat and continued to walk.

"Because you are a smart man. You just need to set your feelings aside and look at this logically."

"I don't need you to tell me what to do." Roger turned and glared at him.

"Someone has to make you see the light."

"And that someone is you, I suppose."

"I have had many people stop me this morning and tell me that someone needs to talk to you. People are worried about you."

"They can stop worrying. I am fine." He started walking again.

"You don't seem fine."

"Why is it you think you know me so well?" Roger turned once more to look at Patrick.

"We have known each other our whole lives. There isn't much I don't know about you."

"If you knew me that well, you would not have voted the way you did."

"I did the right thing."

"You took the easy way out."

"Easy? This is not easy. This is the only place I have ever called home. Do you have any idea how bad it hurt to leave it?"

"Do I have any idea?" Roger stormed up to Patrick now. "This is my baby. My family started this town. I know all too well how much it hurts."

"You think your pain is any worse than anyone else in this city?"

"I think this city is my heart. When it dies, I die." Roger turned again and walked away.

"You are looking at this all wrong!" Patrick yelled at him.

"I'm tired of you telling me how to do things." Roger kept walking.

"Once this is over, we can come back and rebuild the city again. You will have your baby back."

"You don't get it, do you?"

"I don't get you right now."

"I can't leave the city to the trolls. I just can't."

"Well, my friend, it's not like I want to, but for now there isn't another choice."

"There is always another choice."

"What are you going to do? Stay here and defend her alone?"

"I haven't decided yet."

"You are losing it. You will be killed. What happens then?"

Roger kept walking.

"You're not answering because you know I am right!" Patrick yelled as he kept walking.

* * * * *

Lotgren sat at his table when a knock came at his door.

"Come in." He looked up from his dinner.

"Sorry to interrupt, but I have messages for you from Brakac and Deptoe," a young dwarf said as he entered.

"Please come in and deliver your messages." Lotgren motioned him to the table.

"They both send basically the same message."

"Yes."

"Vwnrush is now being run by Alfozmit. Somehow he won the election a month ago and is building his own army of sorts and won't let us anywhere near the city. What do you want us to do?"

"Alfozmit! How did that happen?" Lotgren was almost beside himself. He knew Alfozmit a long time and knew he was a crook and a sneak, just to name a few things. "This is bad news for sure." He looked at the dwarf. "Please send word to the council that I need to meet with them."

"They are waiting for you. Your commanders sent word to them as well. They both are very concerned about what is going on there."

"For good reasons. Let's not keep the council waiting."

They headed out the door and down the path to the apple tree. There he found the council sitting and waiting for him.

"I understand you know why I am here?" Lotgren said. "Thank you for seeing me so quickly."

"You think there is a problem in Vwnrush?" one of the council members said.

"Yes, and since that city could be the races' last stand."

"You want to go and make sure the problem is fixed?" another council member said.

"Alfozmit was elected to run the city," another member said.

"Yes, but his track record makes me question things," Lotgren replied.

"He is not to be trusted," another council member said.

"He has formed his own army of some kind," Lotgren said.

"Yes, this is what bothers us most. Why refuse help?" a council member said.

Lotgren didn't say anything, just looked at them.

"Go find out what you can. If you need help, get it. We need this city secure. If it is not, the other races will blame us as this is our lands."

"Be careful. Alfozmit is very sly," another council member said.

"Thank you. I will leave in the morning." Lotgren turned and left.

"I need you to head back and tell Brakac and Deptoe to meet me at a place called Lazy Lounge in two days. It's just inside the north gate. Tell them to not wear their uniforms. We don't want to be noticed. Now go."

"Yes, sir."

* * * * *

Nonmumi walked west and was having a good time. He felt sure he would make it to the lake by nightfall. He started thinking about Katie. It had been a long time since he had seen her. He wondered if is she was still living there. Would she remember him? He sure remembered her. She was a human he had fallen in love with. Not just a human but a witch on top of that. It was frowned upon, and he had his military career to think about. He hadn't thought about her in a long time, but going to Vwnrush, the memories all came back.

As he walked, he almost didn't notice the rain had stopped as he was deep in thought. It had started to warm up a little even. He did notice the sun dropping in the sky and that he had been going slower than he had thought. He picked up his pace, hoping to still make themselves at the lake by nightfall. As he went, he started feeling like he was being watched. It sent chills up his back, and for the first time ever, he wished he wasn't alone.

"My lady, please watch over me," Nonmumi said out loud, looking to the sky.

He reached the point where the woods and the lake were as close to each other as they came. He decided to make a break for the water. He hoped to find a boat there so he would be safe on the water for the night. He looked around, saw nothing, took a deep breath, and ran. He was open and headed toward the water. He waited to hear something coming after him. His heart was pounding in his ears, and he was breathing hard. He saw a small boat and ran to it, pushed it into the water and jumped in and rowed out some.

"Thank you, my lady. May this water be blessed by you and keep me safe." He put his finger in the water as he said it. He looked back, certain he would see whatever was chasing him, and saw nothing on the beach. Just then, he noticed a shadow seeming to move. He blinked his eyes and saw nothing. He rowed a little more, then felt safe and lay back and slept.

CHAPTER 14

The storm that was looming had only been a few showers and gone. Leigh was standing, looking down at Whiley.

"I should have told him not to touch it." Leigh sighed.

"It's going to be fine. There is a reason it happened. We just have to wait," Felix reassured him.

Leigh went and sat back down. "We are losing a lot of time we don't have." Leigh was frustrated.

"Shh, listen." Felix motioned for him to be quiet. They both listened. "There it is again," Felix said quietly.

Leigh grabbed his sword, not sure what Felix was hearing, but was going to be ready.

"We need to move!" Felix yelled.

"Where?"

"The little rowboat! Go on the water now!"

Leigh picked up Whiley and put him over his shoulder and stumbled out the door. Just then, there was a loud crash at the back of the house. Leigh picked up the pace and had Whiley in the boat, pushing him on to the water.

Felix was waving his hands and muttering.

Leigh looked back. "What are you doing?"

"A spell to confuse whatever is coming. Now bless that water with the sword."

Leigh put the sword in the water. "My lady, bless this water in your name. May you keep us safe so mote it be." He turned the sword out and got ready.

Felix and Leigh were both waiting for what was coming after them. That didn't take long. A troll and a mountain dog. The dog was the size of a horse but built like a dog. They were very quick and agile for their size. The trolls had them as pets. The troll spotted them and pointed, and the mountain dog attacked.

Leigh tightened the grip on his sword, and the magic burst through him, almost overwhelming him. He managed to maintain control for the moment. The fear he had at first now faded as the magic made him feel powerful.

"Get ready!" Felix yelled. Felix muttered again and waved his hands. Suddenly, there was ice under the dog. It caught the dog off guard and sent him skidding.

Leigh, seeing the opportunity, swung and caught the dog across the chest. There was a loud scream. The sword left a huge cut, and there was blood everywhere.

The dog got up and came right after Leigh. Leigh stepped to one side and swung again. He almost severed the dog's left front leg. Again, there was a high-pitched scream. The dog turned again to come for Leigh. He was right there in front of him and ran the sword deep into the dog's chest. As he did, the magic exploded into the dog. The dog howled, and the high-pitched scream came again. A shadow slipped from the dog and into the ground, and the dog fell over, dead.

The troll yelled, and Felix muttered something and waved his hands, and the house fell forward onto the troll.

"Nice," Leigh said, smiling.

"It's not over. That won't kill him. Just bought you some time to catch your breath."

Just then, the troll burst from under the rubble and charged for Leigh.

"Watch out for his club. It has spikes!" Felix yelled.

"Thanks." Leigh took a stance and felt the magic surge through him again. As he got closer, Felix muttered and waved his hands. The dead dog spun and tripped the troll. Leigh swung as the troll went down and got his upper right arm. The sword cut deep into the muscle. There was another loud scream along with the troll yelling.

Leigh went to jump on his back to finish him, but the troll was up and sent him flying. He landed so hard he thought he had broken every bone in his body. The troll was there in seconds, and Leigh rolled to his right just in time. The troll slammed his big foot where his head was. Leigh grabbed the sword tight again, and once again, the magic burst though him, but now he was getting a little more use to it. The troll had his club in his left hand now but was very clumsy with it. Leigh was looking for an opening to kill or hurt him more. The troll lifted the club as he came again.

Felix muttered and waved his hands again, and a tree root came out of the ground. It caught the troll and down he went. Leigh jumped on his back and shoved the sword deep in his back through his heart. The magic exploded into the troll. The troll screamed, and there was the high-pitched scream again. A shadow slipped out and into the ground.

Leigh pulled his sword out and collapsed on the ground.

"Well done." Felix flew over to him.

Leigh was drained from the magic. "Thank you for your help." He barely got out.

"Come, my boy, rest in the boat. It's safer there."

* * * * *

Lor had flown out of the city and down to the southern bay. He had sent word out to those in Juna that he was looking to get a job done. He wanted it done neat with no way to track it back to him. It didn't take long for a response to come back. A man who refused to give his name for now sent someone to meet with him and see what it was he needed done. "I hate it down here," Lor mumbled as he landed. A fish market had burned out a while back, but it had yet to be torn down, and it made the area look very run down. Lor walked slowly toward the building. He was supposed to meet this guy in front of it, and they would talk about what he needed done. He walked slowly; there were homeless who now stayed in the burnt-out building. He had heard that it was a growing problem. Now he saw it firsthand.

"Anything to eat, sir? I haven't eaten in days." One of the homeless came to him.

"Sorry, no." He just kept walking.

"May the goddess bless you." The homeless hawk man called after him.

Lor rolled his eyes and kept walking.

"It's not very nice to not return a blessing, you know," a voice came from the dark. Lor looked to his left, and a man walked out of the shadows.

"And why do you care?" Lor talked down to the man.

"I don't, just making an observation."

"You can keep them to yourself."

"You're a pleasant fellow." The man half smiled.

"I can be when I need to be, but not here."

"Why are you here? You don't belong here."

"If you must know, I am meeting someone here."

"I see, then you must be Lor."

"Yes, how did . . . You are who I am meeting?"

"It would seem so."

"Listen, I don't have time for silly games. I need someone, let's say, disposed of, shall we?"

"And who is that someone?"

"I don't know that I wish to tell you the name right now."

"Well, then you won't get an answer from my boss."

"Who is your boss? Why wouldn't he give his name?"

"The less you know about him, the better. You can't be connected to him."

"OK. The hawk person I want taken out is Curr. I will say no more till I have a meeting with your boss."

"You don't mean—"

"Yes, the one who used to work for me," Lor cut him off.

"Curr, I see. I will tell him. He will get back to you soon."

"Well, make it as soon as possible. I need this done fast." With that, Lor turned, walked a short distance, and flew off.

"He is not very smart, is he?" the man said.

"No, he is not," Curr said as he walked out of the shadows.

"So what is your plan?"

"I have to get him before he tries to get me."

The other man smiled at him.

"He picked the wrong one to mess with this time." Curr smiled as he was formulating a plan in his head.

CHAPTER 15

"Lora, I'm sorry," Rex finally said after not speaking for hours.

They had finally left the city, and Lora saw a secluded bunch of trees and suggested they take a break.

"Sorry for what?" she snapped. "Sorry for grabbing the bow? Sorry for acting like a jerk? Sorry for almost getting us killed? What exactly are you sorry for?"

He stood up from sitting with Tanner under a tree and looked surprised at how she was talking to him.

"What? Nothing to say now?" she blasted him again. She wasn't normally like this, but she was tired and scared. She had no idea what she should do, so yelling at Rex was all she could think of.

"Just sorry," he finally said.

Lora sighed. "Get over here so I can try and mend your wing."

He looked at her, not sure what to do.

"I'm done yelling. Get over here." She opened her pack. "My mother sent along a few things in case one of us got hurt."

"Good thinking."

"Are you two going to keep fighting? My head is killing me," Tanner said as he fluttered his eyes and tried to shake the cobwebs from his head.

"Tanner!" Lora darted to him.

"My wing," Rex complained.

Lora glared at him.

"I'll wait, not a problem." Rex hung his head.

"Where are we?" Tanner asked as he sat up.

"About fifteen minutes outside the city. We had to stop. We are exhausted," Lora told him as she helped him sit better. "How are you?"

"I'm fine. How did we get here?"

"What do you remember?"

"Those guys stopped us and . . . " He glared at Rex. "Why did you grab the bow?"

"Because he is an ass," Lora said before Rex could respond. Rex chose to be silent. "What else?" Lora asked.

"I grabbed the bow, and the magic ran through me and took over. Then I was with the goddess." He stopped for a minute, then he grabbed her. "The darkness is coming fast. It's bad."

"Calm down. It's OK," Lora was reassuring him.

"Wait, what happened to the guys that stopped us? How did you get out of that?"

Lora and Rex looked at each other. Then Lora told him, in detail, of what happened.

"The magic is strong. The goddess told me, 'Don't try and control it, but don't let it control you. You must work in harmony.'"

Rex handed him some dried fruit. "I'm sorry. You are the chosen, and after what I saw, I'm glad I'm not."

Lora and Tanner just looked at him. "Rex, you must be an important part or the goddess would not have let you come along," Tanner said, then ate.

Lora was shocked at that statement.

"Thank you." Rex smiled.

"Why don't you get some sleep while I keep watch?" Tanner said as he stood up.

"Are you sure you are OK?" Lora asked.

"Yes, where is my bow?"

"Right here." Lora took it off her back and handed it to him.

"Good, you two sleep for a couple of hours, then we are off to the temple."

Lora mended Rex's wing, and they slept. Tanner sat, watching and thinking about his talk with the goddess.

* * * * *

Alastrine and his company had a good time. The day was sunny and warm. At first they were passing several families going to the city where it was safe. None of them had seen any trolls, but everyone was scared. By late day, they had stopped seeing people. They rode till after dinner when they spotted a farmhouse.

"We should stop here for lunch. There is a small barn. We can keep the horses there and go on foot," Alastrine was telling his men.

Then to their surprise, the door of the house opened, and a middle-aged man and a younger man came out.

"Can we help you?" the old man asked as he held a long sword.

"Not here to cause problems, sir. We just thought this place would be abandoned and we were going to stop and rest," Alastrine said, holding his hand up.

"Well, it's not, and me and my son aren't leaving, troll or no troll, understand?" They were both tall and well-built from working on the farm. They both carried a long sword and seemed to know how to use them.

"We will move along," Alastrine said as he waved.

The son whispered to the father.

"Hold, are you the keeper Alastrine?" the father yelled as they were leaving.

"Yes," Alastrine said as he stopped his horse.

"Then by all means, stop and rest. Please." The father gave his sword to his son to hold. He came off the porch to meet Alastrine.

"Thank you, but we don't want to be a bother," Alastrine replied.

"No bother. Have you had dinner yet? Come, eat," he was saying as he came up to his horse. "I'm James. That is my son, Will. He noticed your cloak. Sorry I didn't."

"Not a problem, James." Alastrine got off his horse and shook his hand. "Nice to meet you and your son."

"The pleasure is all ours. Are you going after the trolls? Terrible what they have done." James turned and led the way back to the house. "Will help the others tend to the horses, then bring them in to eat." James led Alastrine into the house.

Will grabbed Alastrine's horse, and the others dismounted and followed him to the barn.

James directed Alastrine to a large table that could sit a dozen easily.

"Big table for just two," Alastrine said as he sat down.

"No," James laughed. "The wife and nine other children went to Moray to be safe."

"Then why didn't you two go?"

"I have worked too hard to let trolls or anyone take it away from me." James sat down heavily at the table.

The others were walking back from the barn as James stood and looked out the window.

"Small group to be taking on the trolls," James observed.

"Not taking them on as much as slowing them down so the cities can be better prepared."

"Prepared? How do you prepare for trolls?" James turned and looked at Alastrine.

"The chosen ones need to get to the temple and restore the balance," Alastrine said.

"That will take time we don't have," James said, feeling a little angry now.

The door opened and the others came in.

"Will, help me set the table and feed our guest." James got up, all smiles. They feed them some bread, fruit, and dried meat. When they were close to done, Alastrine pulled James to the side.

"I would try and talk you into going where it is safe, but I don't think you will listen," Alastrine said, looking at him, hoping he was wrong.

"I'm not going."

"I need a favor then."

"Anything, just ask."

"I want to leave the horses here. We need to sneak in and out of places and can't do that with the horses."

"They will be here waiting for you when you come back."

"Thank you, my friend. May the goddess bless and keep you and your son safe."

"Thank you. May she do the same for you and your company."

"Now I will do you a favor. Where are your swords?"

"Over there is the corner. Why?"

Alastrine grabbed his water and went to the swords and blessed them. "That should help in your fight if there is one."

"You are to kind. Thank you."

The two hugged and walked back to where everyone else was.

"Gentlemen, we go on foot from here. James has offered to watch over the horses till our return. Now we must go, get your things together. We leave in five minutes." Alastrine turned to James. "Thank you, my friend, for everything."

They all got their things together, said their thanks and good-byes, and headed down the road on foot now.

CHAPTER 16

Lark called the meeting to order. He had asked the other seven members of the council to meet without Lor.

"Is this OK for us to do?" Zak, the youngest member of the council, asked.

Zak had only been in the council a very short time, and Lor had taken him under his wing. More so that he had an ally, not that he cared for Zak. Zak had a brown beck that matched his deep brown eyes. His hair was dirty blond, and his smile could melt your heart. He had a heart of gold but often got used by others.

"Lor is too busy worrying about being liked. We need to be ready for what is coming," Lark said sharply. "We don't have time for his games. Not to mention he questioned the goddess and believes his son will save us all."

The rest of the council agreed, and Lark smiled at Zak. "Bren, you are the head of our army. Tell the rest what you told me." Lark motioned for him to speak.

"The trolls will get after the temple. That is where the chosen ones need to do the magic. If you know your history, that is where the crystal that the four stones direct their energy through. The elves have a small company there, but not enough for when the trolls attack it in large numbers. I would think the elves and dwarfs are sending backup there as I am sure they are thinking the same thing. The humans have problems of their own. Word has it trolls are already attacking them, so they are tied up defending themselves right now, not that they have much of an army anyway."

"So get to the point already," Stan interrupted.

"What I propose is we send two companies to help back them up. If the temple is lost, we are done."

"Does that leave us weak here?" Kam asked.

"This island is most likely the last place they will come. If we have to defend it, we are already done."

"What does Lor think?" Zak asked.

Annoyed by that question, Lark barked, "He thinks his son is going to save everyone. Now we only need Lor if there is a tie vote. So let's vote. All in favor, raise your right hand."

Everyone put up their hands except Zak, who slowly put his hand up after everyone glared at him.

"Fine, it is unanimous. Bren, get to work on that now. Meeting adjourned."

They all shook hands and were leaving the hall when a small boy stopped Lark.

"Sir, are you Lark?" the boy asked.

"Yes, boy, why?" Lark looked at the others. "Go on, I will talk to you tomorrow."

Turning to the boy, he asked, "What is it you need?"

"I'm to give this to you." The boy handed him a note.

"Who sent this?" Lark asked the boy, and the boy turned and ran.

Lark stood looking confused, but after a couple of seconds, he opened the note.

Lark,

If you want dirt on Lor, and finally get rid of
him, meet me by the burnt-out fishing market at
the southern bay in one hour.

Lark looked on the back and then at the note again. No one had signed it.

* * * * *

"Look what I got." A fourth troll came up behind Arastrude and O, holding Dagrel by his ankle and his sword in the other hand. "What a cute sword." The troll held the sword up and looked at it.

"Let my friend go!" O yelled.

One of the trolls grabbed Arastrude. "She friend too?" The troll laughed.

"Yes, they are O's friends. They are good. Let them go."

One of the other trolls shoved O. "They are not friends. Trolls have no friends," he said as O fell to the ground.

"This one"—the troll held up Dagrel—"is hard to hold on to." Just then, Dagrel swung himself up and grabbed the sword out of the troll's other hand.

The magic shot through Dagrel, and he brought the sword up and drove it into the troll's chest. The magic exploded into the troll. There was a high-pitched scream that made them all look.

O took the opportunity to tackle the troll holding Arastrude, sending him flying to the ground. Arastrude stumbled off to the side.

The troll that held Dagrel fell dead and a shadow slipped into the ground. Dagrel sprung to his feet as one of the trolls came for him.

O was stomping on the head of the troll he tackled, yelling, "You not hurt O's friends, bad troll."

The fourth troll looked confused and didn't move right away.

As the troll that came after Dagrel got close, he leaped onto a small boulder and the troll stumbled by him. The troll turned in time to see Dagrel coming out of the boulder with his sword up. Dagrel planted the sword and kept it into the troll's chest. The magic burst into the troll, and again there was a high-pitched scream along with the troll's scream as he fell dead almost on top of the other dead troll, and a shadow slipped into the ground.

The forth troll had gone after O, who was still stomping on the head of the troll he tackled. Dagrel was on the back of the fourth troll in seconds. The troll shook and tried to throw him off and finally threw Dagrel to the ground. Dagrel hit the ground and rolled to his feet as the troll turned to come after him. Dagrel sidestepped him and cut deep into the troll's left leg as he passed. The troll yelled in pain, grabbed a large rock, turned, and threw it at Dagrel. He jumped out of the way just in time as he almost got hit in the head. Dagrel turned to get up.

"Look out, he's coming!" Arastrude yelled at him.

Dagrel tucked and rolled out of the troll's path and was back on his feet in seconds. Dagrel spotted a large rock and ran to it. The troll came at the rock from the other direction. Dagrel hit the rock with both feet, springing himself into the troll, where he drove his sword deep into the troll's chest. There was another loud scream and the troll lay dead, and a shadow slipped into the ground.

Dagrel picked himself up, walked over to where O was still stomping away, and drove his sword into the back of the troll he was stomping on. A loud scream came, and the troll stopped moving.

Dagrel pulled his sword free of the troll and stumbled backward. The magic had taken a lot out of him.

O grabbed Dagrel before he fell. O carried him back to where he had been sleeping and put him down.

"Thank you, O. You are a good friend," Dagrel said, exhausted.

"Me good troll," O said.

"Yes, good troll." And Dagrel passed out.

"Looks like you and me on watch, O," Arastrude said as she covered Dagrel up.

CHAPTER 17

After Elyon and Captain Folmar had moved Luvon closer to the water, he had passed out. The magic had drained him, and Elyon sat by him and watched over him.

"Luvon," a soft voice came.

He heard his name; he thought he did anyway.

"Luvon."

There it was again. He was sure this time.

"Who is there?" he said softly as he opened his eyes. He was no longer at the river with the others. He was in his tree house. How he loved it there. That is where he would go to meditate, and if he could be there, that is where he would think of when meditating. It was so peaceful there, and his friends were there with him all the time. It was the best place in the world.

"Luvon, you know me."

"I do?" he said as he looked around. It was odd no one but him was there.

"Luvon, I chose you."

"Goddess Atla, my lady."

"Luvon, you did well today."

"I'm scared. The magic is strong."

"Luvon, I chose you. You can handle it."

"But it's nothing like elf magic. It scared me today."

"That will pass. All you have to do is work with it."

"How?"

"Don't try and control it. Don't let it control you."

"My lady, why did you pick me?"

"You look after your friends like they are your children. You care deeply for others, some you don't even know very well. You have a good soul, that is why."

"I don't know if I can do what you need me to."

"If you fail, the shadows will win and those you care for will suffer."

"I don't want that."

"That is why I picked you. Now go back to your friends and restore the balance. It is the only way."

He closed his eye even though he didn't want to.

"The boats are as good as they are going to get, I'm afraid," one of the bowmen said to Captain Folmar and Elyon.

"Then it will have to do," Captain Folmar said.

Luvon opened his eyes slowly.

"He is waking up," Elyon said, smiling.

"About time, boy. You OK?" Captain Folmar asked.

"Yeah, he shook his head a little. How long was I out?" he asked as he sat up.

"Several hours. It's after dinner now, but the boats just got fixed," Elyon said.

"Yes, and we need to get going. We lost a lot of time," Captain Folmar said.

"You two." He pointed to two bowmen. "Take a boat and go inform the king of what has happened. He needs to be warned."

"Yes, sir," they both said and pushed off in one of the boats and started paddling back upstream.

"You." He pointed to the injured bowmen. "You will ride with me, Elyon, and Luvon. You, other three, take the other boat and follow us. Keep your eyes open for anything."

The other two boats were pushed off, and all got in and started toward the temple once again

* * * * *

"John, can I have a minute with you?" Alex asked as the men he asked to meet him arrived at themselves docks. John was a short small-framed man with black hair and brown eyes and dark skin. He was the best woodworker in the city. Alex pulled him to the side.

"I need you to work with the ladies at the meeting hall," Alex said.

"OK, what am I doing?"

"Building tents that can hold twenty people, lots of them. The ladies will sew. I need you to do the design and poles or whatever works."

"That's a lot." He was already figuring things in his head.

"Put the word out that you need help. Now these need to be able to travel easy."

"I'll go to see the ladies first and work out a plan."

"This needs to happen fast," Alex urged.

"OK, not a problem." John turned and headed for the hall.

Alex turned back to the others.

"Pete, you run the docks. This is what I need you to do."

Pete was an older man who made sure things ran smoothly at the docks. He was six feet tall with full beard, shoulder-length salt-and-pepper hair. No one gave him trouble.

"I need as many fishing boats turned into passenger boats as we can and still have fish coming in to feed everyone."

"That's a tall order, Alex." Pete rubbed his chin.

"The boats need to be made stronger to take the rough waters if we have to make an escape that way to Lorn."

"I'll work on it and update you as often as I can."

"I'll need you to work with Jake. Jake, I need you to ration food and water. We are making tents and sending groups of eighty at a time east over the mountains."

They all looked shocked.

"The trolls and the shadows are coming. We have to be prepared for the worst."

"It's late summer, the supplies are low. The farmers would be bringing things in within the next couple of weeks." Jake sighed.

"Talk to those at the warehouse. See if we can get some of the closer farms and save what we can. Be safe in doing so. Do the best you can."

"OK, I'm on it," Jake said, already running numbers in his head. Jake was a short, skinny, blond with blue eyes. He could run figures in his head faster than anyone. That's why Alex had him keep track of the cities' food stocks and how much to give out.

"Now, Phil." Phil was a balding man who had gotten a little heavy in his later years, but you still didn't want to mess with him. His hands were all calloused from working with them all his life. He was in charge of maintaining the cities' walls.

"Phil, we need to reinforce the main wall and put another wall and traps in front of that. Anything that will slow the trolls down and take out as many as we can."

"That's a lot of work. Going to need a lot of help."

"I know, but we need it done."

"I have a couple of guys. We will get working on plans and building right away."

"Arron, you are the head of our defense."

Arron was young but already the best bowman and swordsman in town. He was medium built and in great shape with black hair and brown eyes.

"I need you to make sure weapons are blessed and make lots of them. Train as many as you can, bowmen more than others. When they come, we need to be ready."

"Yes, sir. Getting right on it."

"All of you, put the word out in the city of the help you need. It will come. Everyone is scared of the trolls. They will do what it takes to be safe. Gentlemen, I have faith in you. Update me often. I am going to make sure my wife has taken a break and I'll get something to eat myself. I will check back in with you in a couple of hours."

He looked at them each one at a time.

"Many lives will be affected by what we accomplish here. We may not save our city in the end, but we can save as many as we can and take as many of them out as we can. Time is short, maybe shorter than we know. So don't waste any of it. Now be off, and may the goddess look over what we are doing and bless it."

He shook each of their hands as they left and wondered if anything they are doing will stop the trolls or give enough time to the chosen to restore the balance.

CHAPTER 18

Lark paced back and forth in his living room, reading the note over and over. He was unsure if he was being set up or not. He couldn't afford not to go if the note was real. Finally, he got mad, crumpled up the note, threw it in the trash, grabbed his short sword, and went out the door.

Summer was coming to an end, and the nights were getting cooler. He got to the edge of the city rather fast as he wasn't sure what time it was and didn't want to miss the meeting. If there was one, he thought.

He spread his wings and gently glided down from the city to the southern bay. As he landed, the little fishing village was going to sleep and there were not many lights on. He landed a couple blocks from the meeting place. Pulled out his sword and slowly made his way there, checking every nook and cranny for any signs of trouble. But there was none; he got to the burnt-out fishers' market with no trouble.

"Hello," Lark said, looking around. He was starting to feel like he shouldn't have come.

"You're late," a voice came from the dark.

Lark pulled his sword up, ready to fight.

"You don' t need that," the voice came again. Then someone stepped out of the shadows.

"You!" Lark spat. "I can't waste my time listening to the likes of you."

"Why not?" Curr asked.

"Because most of what you say are lies, designed to help you in whatever it is you need at that time," Lark spat back.

"No reason to be angry." Curr smiled. "I mean, for the most part you are right."

"I'm not angry," Lark replied, calmer.

"OK, do you want to know why I ask you here?"

"I'm here, so you might as well tell me." Lark put his sword away.

"I can give you the proof you need that Lor had his father killed."

"Turning yourself in?" Lark laughed.

"Do you want the information or not?"

"Yes, but what is in it for you?" Lark asked calmly.

"Think you know me well, do you?" Curr folded his arms and leaned against one of the burnt beams.

"Know your type. You don't do anything without strings attached."

"For the most part, true enough, and yes there is something in it for me."

"I knew it." Lark smiled.

"The price is small." Curr returned the smile.

"Let's just cut to the chase. What do you know?"

"Lor hired me to kill his father. It was supposed to look like a suicide."

"Why are you telling me this? I could take you in now."

"But I'm not the one you want."

"He will say you're lying."

"What if I could get him to say that he did it?"

"That would be great. How?" Lark was still unsure.

"Well, he and I had a little disagreement, and now he has contacted, let's say, a colleague of mine."

"Yes, let's say that." Lark half rolled his eyes.

"He wants him to kill me. Says I know too much." Curr half laughed.

"OK, keep going."

"He is meeting said colleague tomorrow night here."

"What are you thinking?" Lark asked, already thinking the same thing.

"You and some authorities be here listening. My colleague will get him to say everything."

"What do you want in return?"

"I will make a statement confirming what he says. For you making sure my wings don't get clipped and no tower jail."

"What makes you think I can make such a deal?"

"Do you want Lor?"

Lark took a deep breath. "Deal." They shook hands.

"Be here just before sunset. Lor will be here shortly after that." Curr smiled and walked back into the shadows.

* * * * *

"Whiley, come down and eat breakfast. You're going to be late," Came a lady's voice.

Whiley opened his eyes looked around. He was in a room, lying in a bed.

"Whiley, are you listening?" the ladies voice came again.

"Yes, Mom," he said, not sure really why.

"OK, then get moving. Your friends will all be waiting for you."

Whiley sat up, very confused. Where was he? He got up and got dressed in clothes that were lying on a chair.

"I put clothes on your chair. Hope they are fine."

"They are. Thanks, Mom." He said *mom* again. Why?

He got dressed and went downstairs where there were eggs and toast waiting for him. No signs of the lady he kept calling mom. He sat down and slowly began to eat. Then he thought, *I must be dreaming, wishing this is where I was, but it seems so real.*

"This is what you always wanted, isn't it? This is the place where you thought you would always feel safe," a soft voice came.

"To have a mom and a home? Yes, very much," he said out loud, but not sure to who.

"You have helped many younger children have this life," the soft voice came again.

"Who are you? How do you know me?" Whiley was very confused now.

"You know me, Whiley. Just think."

Whiley sat for a moment. "My lady, the goddess." He was excited.

"Yes, Whiley."

"Wait, am I dead?"

"No, I brought you here."

"Why?"

"You have questions. Ask them."

"They don't matter now. I'm here and I'm not leaving." Whiley smiled.

"Ask."

"OK, my lady. Why did you pick me?"

"You did what you could to help those children find homes. You thought no one knew when just about everyone knew. You did it without looking for anything in return."

"That's why?" Whiley was still confused.

"You have a good soul, Whiley. You care a great deal about others."

"Will that help me?"

"Yes."

"But I want to stay here." Whiley felt so at peace here.

"Look out the window, Whiley."

Whiley stood and looked; it was sunny, but off in the distance, dark clouds were rolling in fast.

"A storm?" Whiley asked, knowing that was wrong.

"Worse."

"The shadows," Whiley whispered.

"Yes, they come to take this all away. From you and those you helped."

"I have to help stop it," he said without thinking about it.

"Yes."

"But the magic, will it work for me?"

"Don't try and control it. Work in harmony with it and it will work."

"How do I get back?"

"Go out the front door and help your friends."

Whiley raced to the door, took one last look, and opened it.

Whiley's eyes fluttered as he opened them. He was in a rowboat on a little pond.

CHAPTER 19

A knock came at the door. Roger looked up. He was sitting in a chair in a small office in his house.

"Come in," he said, half choked up.

"Sir." A small boy opened the door. "You have a visitor."

"Who is it?" He really wasn't in the mood for visitors.

"A messenger from Moray."

He sat up a bit more now. "Send him in." *Maybe Alastrine has some good news.*

"Sir, before I go. My family is leaving, so I can't be your page anymore." The boy looked sad. "I will miss you, sir."

"It's fine, my boy. Go with your family. I will see you again." He smiled, knowing that may not be true.

He let the other boy in and left.

"Sir, I have a message from Alex for you." He handed him an envelope.

"Thank you, my boy." Roger took the note and read it, then laid it down.

"Sir, are you OK?" The boy asked. Roger looked at him, his eyes all red from lack of sleep.

"No, son, I'm not. What is your name, son?"

"Barney. Anything I can do for you, sir?" Barney was not very tall and was skinny, with brown hair and brown eyes.

"Are you to go back to Moray?"

"No, I'm to go onto Lorn."

"I see. Follow me, Barney."

He followed Roger out of his house down the small streets that were deserted.

"Where is everyone?" Barney asked.

"Gone. Trolls have scared everyone. The council doesn't think we can defend this city. So most are gone or soon will be gone to Lorn." Roger stopped at a door. "Just follow me in and have a seat." They walked in, and Barney sat down like he was asked to. Roger went over to a long table where another man was packing up boxes.

"Look, Patrick, a message from Moray."

Patrick took the note and read it.

"Why are you showing me this?"

"The men are staying to try and defend their city as long as they can."

"Your point?"

"Why can't we do the same here?"

"Moray has the ocean to flee on if they need to. What do we have?"

"Maybe we won't have to flee. What if we hold them off?"

"Not likely. We have had this talk. I am sorry you can' t come to terms with the facts, but the rest of us have."

"Don't know why I wasted my breath. I keep hoping my friend will show up, but I guess not." Roger turned to leave.

"I am your friend. Sorry you don't believe that."

Roger just kept walking and motioned for Barney to follow him as he walked by him. Barney did so without question.

"It's late. You can spend the night if you like. I have room and then you can head for Lorn in the morning."

"OK, sir. Thank you," Barney said.

"Would you walk with me?" Roger was choking back tears.

"Sure, sir."

They walked down two different streets and ended up by the river.

"See that small house with a little shop attached to the side?" Roger pointed to the other side of the river.

"Yes, sir." Barney nodded.

"That was my great-great-grandfather's. He started this city. This was his dream, to start another city, because Moray and Lorn had gotten so big. This was a growing city with a lot going for it." Tears started coming again.

"You OK, sir?" Barney rubbed his back lightly, not knowing was else to do.

"Just had to come see it again. We can go back to my house now. We will eat, then get some sleep." Roger turned and walked back up the street. "Then you can leave in the morning," he added as Barney followed.

"What about you, sir?"

"Well, I'm here a couple of days to make sure everyone is gone and the boats are filled and gone. Then I'll be the last to leave."

"I have no family, sir. I would be glad to stay and help you." Barney felt bad for him and wanted to help.

"That would be nice. Thank you, son." Roger smiled at him, and they went back to his house and ate. Roger showed him his room and then went to bed himself.

* * * * *

"Bhargel, sir, there are more troll tracks over here." One of the scouts had seen tracks in the mud earlier that morning, and they had been tracking them ever since.

"It seemed they were going to the temple, but now they seemed to be going away from the temple." The scout reported.

"They may have just gotten confused. Let's continue to follow them," Bhargel said. "We need to see what they are doing and get rid of a problem before it gets bigger."

They continued following the tracks as the sun rose.

"Sir, up here!" a scout yelled.

Bhargel and the others ran to the scout.

"What is it?"

"Blood, sir." They looked where the scout was pointing. There was a blood that seemed to be running from somewhere in the woods.

"OK, men, weapons ready. Spread out." Bhargel pointed to where he wanted everyone. "Move slowly. We don't know what's up ahead."

They only walked for a short time, and they saw two dead trolls.

"Check to see—" Bhargel was cut off.

"Friends, more friends." Bhargel looked to his left to see who was yelling just in time to see O, who was already on top of him, picking him up and bear hugging him.

"It's OK!" Arastrude yelled, running after him. The others had weapons ready. "He is a friend."

"Put me down!" Bhargel yelled.

"OK." He sat him down and patted him on the head. "You O's friend?"

"What's going on here?" Bhargel demanded.

"Put your weapons down. He is a friend!" Dagrel yelled, running out from the trees.

"Do not pat me on the head!" Bhargel said, swatting at O's hand. "Now tell me what's going on, and where is Nonmumi?"

Dagrel started explaining what had happened and where Nonmumi was. O and Arastrude chimed in here and there.

"The goddess sent a troll to help," Bhargel said, shaking his head.

"I was unsure myself till we were attacked and he stood with us."

"O good troll." O smiled as they all looked at him.

"I'm worried about Nonmumi. The woods have a bad feeling about them," Dagrel said.

"I agree. I'm sending my men to find him. I'll go with you to the temple," Bhargel said. "I'll leave me second in command to watch the woods."

He called his men over and gave them orders to find Nonmumi and help him find the humans and get them to the temple. Bhargel looked at the troll O stomped and shook his head.

"Bad troll," O said, looking at him.

"Yes, O, bad troll," Bhargel said.

"O good troll."

"Yes, O, it seems so." Bhargel smiled at him.

"Sir, we are ready and going to head out now," one of the scouts said.

"OK, may the goddess be with you." They shook hands, and the nine went after Nonmumi.

"We should be off too," Bhargel said to the others.

The four headed east toward the temple.

CHAPTER 20

Lora woke before Rex and sat beside Tanner.

"What happened when you were passed out?" Lora asked.

"The goddess talked to me," Tanner said after a few moments.

"What did she say?" Lora asked, excited.

"The magic is strong, and we have to work with it." Tanner sighed, still trying to make sense of what he was told.

"What does that mean?" Lora asked, confused.

"Not sure." Tanner shrugged.

"Did she say anything else?"

He thought for a moment

"The shadows are coming fast. We have to get to the temple." Tanner looked at her straight in the face. "It's bad. I'll be honest, I'm scared. There is a lot riding on what we do."

"Are you OK?" Lora put her hand on his shoulder.

"Yeah, but we should get moving." Tanner got up and woke up Rex.

"Rex, sorry, but we need to get moving."

"What? Oh, OK." Rex struggled to wake up.

"How is your wing?" Lora asked.

Rex went to move it, and his face told the story.

"Still hurts."

"We may have to follow the river through the mountains," Tanner said "We can eat while we walk." Tanner turned and started walking north.

"Is he OK?" Rex asked as he and Lora were catching up to Tanner.

"I'm not sure," Lora said with a look of concern.

They followed the river all afternoon. They saw very few people. The people they saw warned them of the trolls though none of them had seen any.

"We've been pushing hard all morning. I am in a lot of pain. Can we rest for a few?" Rex complained.

"Fine, only for a few," Tanner replied.

Lora looked at Rex's wing.

"Tanner, his wing is swollen bad," Lora said.

Tanner looked. "There is a small waterfall there. Let's bless the water and let the water run over his wing."

They went to the water. Tanner put the end of the bow in the water and blessed it. Lora helped Rex sit and let the water run over it. Tanner laid his stuff with Lora's on the bank and got in to help with Rex.

"That feels good," Rex sighed.

They were still working with his wing when they heard noise by their things. They looked over and saw two large prairie dogs on their things. They laughed until the dogs grabbed the bow.

"They are taking the bow!" Tanner yelled as he rushed to get out of the water followed by Lora. They got to their things as a third prairie dog was grabbing the bag with the stone.

"No, you don't." Lora grabbed the bag and was surprised how good of a grip the dog had. "Let it go!" Lora jerked the bag, and water from her wings hit the prairie dog. It screamed and let go and ran away.

Lora was shocked. Then it hit her. The shadows.

"Rex, it's the shadows." Rex was following Tanner, who was flying much better and faster, chasing after the bow. Lora got into her pack, got a small bowl, filled it with the blessed water, and flew after the other. She caught them as Tanner was trying to get his bow from the dogs. She dumped the water on the dogs. They screamed and let go, then ran into a hole close by.

Rex caught up to them. Tanner looked confused.

Lora held up the bowl. "Blessed water."

"Shadows," Tanner replied.

* * * * *

Nasir burst in on the king as he was eating lunch. Ayre sat without saying a word, but his face showed the shock of the intrusion.

"Your Majesty, please forgive me, but one of the boats that was the with the chosen ones is back."

Ayre rose. "What? Why?"

"I don't know. Your Majesty was sent for you and told to hurry." Nasir was out of breath from running the whole way.

"Take me to it now." Ayre threw his napkin on the table.

"Yes, Your Majesty, follow me."

Nasir led the king down to the docks where the boats had left the day before. There was one of the boats. It was broken in places; scratch marks covered it. Two bowmen were lying on the ground, bloody and cut badly.

"What happened?" Ayre asked, looking at both of them, but neither could answer. "Get them to the palace. Set up beds for them and get them help. I will talk to them there."

There were two stretchers already there, and the elves were whisked away. Ayre took a last look at the boat and followed after the elves.

Ayre was sitting in his study, waiting to talk to the elves and looking through books about the shadows. A knock came at the door.

"Enter," Ayre almost snapped.

"You called, Your Majesty?" Nasir entered softly.

"Yes, my boy, I need you to get Ailred here for me and find out how soon I can see the two elves that came back. Also find Ryo. I need him as well."

"Yes, Your Majesty." Nasir turned to leave.

"Oh, and, Nasir, thank you." Ayre gave him a smile.

"You're welcome, Your Majesty." He left with a smile on his face, off to do what was asked of him. He found Ailred, who was on his way to see the king anyway. He had been told of themselves, the boat, and the two elves.

Ailred was the head of the military. He was older than Ayre, and he remembered when Ayre's father was king. He had red hair that was graying now and green eyes. His tall, slender frame was starting to hunch over a little with age, but he was still able to get around as well as most half his age. Ayre often turned to him for advice, and now he would again.

Nasir had to go almost to the end of the city to find Ryo's house. It was in the northern part of the city. His house had an odd roof; it looked like a crooked cone. Nasir knocked on the door.

"Ah, Nasir, my boy. OK, I'm ready," Ryo said as he answered the door. Ryo had been around longer than anyone could really remember. He was short with blond hair and blue eyes and very light on his feet. And he was the elf who advised the king on elf magic.

"Ready for what?" Nasir looked confused; he hadn't said anything yet.

"To go see the king. I know he sent you for me."

"Yes, of course." Nasir smiled; he had forgotten how good Ryo was at knowing things before they happen. Ryo followed Nasir to the palace.

"The king is waiting—"

"For me in the study, yes, thank you, Nasir," Ryo finished Nasir's sentence.

Nasir went to check on the two injured elves. Their injuries were worse than they looked. There were many broken bones, and they had to be given something to help them rest so the bones could be set. So for now they were still unable to answer any questions.

Nasir went to the study and knocked on the door.

"Enter," Ayre said.

"Your Majesty, the elves are hurt much worse than was thought. It may be morning until they can talk."

"Thank you, Nasir. Keep me updated."

Nasir nodded and left.

"Gentlemen, we can't wait till morning to find out what happened," Ayre said to the other two. "It is obvious that the shadows are much closer to the city than anyone thought. We must be careful. Shadows can possess anything with a weak mind," Ayre said, still not believing what he was saying was happening.

"How close do you think the shadows are?" Ailred asked.

"They could be in this room," Ryo said. "We have to make sure the chosen ones are safe."

"Ryo is right. We have to make sure the chosen are safe." Ayre paced. "Send scouts and make sure their weapons are blessed and they have blessed water."

"Yes, Your Majesty." Ailred turned and left.

"Ryo, we need magical help," Ayre said.

"Elf magic is no match to the goddess's magic," Ryo said flatly.

"We have to make the most of what we have."

"OK, I'm teaching a few elves. We will do what we can," Ryo assured him.

"No, just you. Too many hands in the pot gives too many chances for the shadows to creep in."

"OK, just me."

"Thank you, Ryo. I'll be in contact with you as soon as I talk to the elves from the boat."

"OK, I'll go see the elves as well. Maybe there is some magic I can do to help them."

"Thank you, Ryo, and may the goddess bless us and keep us safe."

Ayre smiled as Ryo left, an odd one he was. He was the only elf that can get away with not addressing him properly because he and his father were best friends and he never addressed his father properly, so why should he be any different? He didn't do it out of disrespect; he was a friend and didn't think he had to, and that was fine.

CHAPTER 21

Lotgren got to Vwnrush's north gate and was surprised to find you had to go through a questioning before you could enter. He waited his turn in line, and when he got to the gate, a man stopped him.

"What is your business in the city?" he asked.

"Meeting up with some old friends here."

"How long are you staying?"

"Just a day. Just catching up."

He looked at Lotgren. "The short sword is all you carry."

"Yes, just for protection."

"Mmm, OK, you may pass. I'll expect you back here tomorrow at this time. Make sure you follow the curfew. Don't want to have to lock you up."

"Curfew in this city?" Lotgren was stunned.

"Yes, the new governor put it in place."

"OK, I will thank you." Lotgren walked into the city and was shocked at how many places had closed and were boarded up. He walked to the Lazy Lounge and was glad to see it was still open. He walked inside and found Brakac and Deptoe waiting for him at a table. He walked over and sat down.

"Just act like we are friends, OK?" Lotgren said softly.

"Hey, how about that screening coming in?" Deptoe said as Lotgren sat down.

"I was told the governor just started that this week," Brakac added.

"Anyone knows why?"

"Some say he is looking for Nonmumi, has a score to settle. The governor says that Nonmumi is working with the trolls. We think he is after those with Nonmumi." Brakac winked, not wanting to bring up the chosen.

"So what is happening in the city?" Lotgren asked.

"A lot of shop owners have pledged their allegiance to the governor and have closed their stores and became part of his so-called police force," Deptoe added.

"A lot of people are saying once they pledge their allegiance, they change and are weird. You know what I am thinking," Brakac said.

"We are getting looked at. Maybe we should go for a walk." Deptoe nodded his head toward the bar where a man in a uniform was watching them.

They got up and left, and the man followed them with his eyes as they left.

"What else is going on?" Lotgren asked as they started walking.

"Well, those who haven't joined the force are scared once friends not treat them like they hardly know them. Several have been arrested for silly things, and when asked to join the force, they say no. They stay locked up or disappear altogether," Brakac said.

"Some are starting to flee the city," Deptoe added.

"Then something had to be done. This is probably where the final stand will take place if there is one," Lotgren said.

"Hey, you guys," a voice came from a small alley.

They all looked down the alley and didn't notice anyone at first.

"I'm here by the trash. Come here fast."

They went down the alley, ready to fight if needed.

"They are looking for you, you know." A small man sat on the ground. He was half starved and very weak.

"Who is?" Lotgren asked.

"The police force."

"Why?"

"They know who you are. You are dwarf soldiers." The man smiled.

"Now why would they think that?"

"They don't think they know." He smiled at them.

"You need to go. Get help. The governor is bad." The man shook his head.

"Thanks for the warning, but we are not who you think we are." Lotgren smiled.

They walked out of the alley and looked at each other.

"I think we should split up. Head back to your units and prepare to take this governor down. I will be in touch," Lotgren said.

"OK," they both said, and they all headed off in different directions.

* * * * *

Alastrine and his party made their way along the mountains. The daylight had started to fade, and their pace slowed. They had not seen any signs of the trolls or any destruction from them. That made Alastrine feel good. They haven't made it very far.

"Alastrine, sir." Ron, one of the bowmen, walked up beside him.

"Yes, mmmm." Alastrine was trying to think.

"Ron, sir."

"What is it, Ron?"

"Several of the men are feeling uneasy. I think there may be shadows nearby," Ron said, looking at Alastrine for confirmation.

"You are very aware of what's around you. That's a good thing. I've been thinking that we are being watched," Alastrine agreed.

"It's going to be dark soon. What are we going to do?" Ron pressed on.

"I've been looking for a safe spot that we can defend if we have to," Alastrine admitted.

"There are some caves up ahead." Ron pointed toward a section of the mountains.

"We could get trapped in a cave," Alastrine protested.

"The ones I know have several exits," Ron offered.

"That would work. Lead the way, my good man," Alastrine said.

Ron led the way up a small hill side to an opening of a cave.

"This will be the easiest one to defend. There are two ways out, and they both came out at the base of the mountain," Ron explained to Alastrine.

"How do you know all this?" Alastrine asked.

"Grew up and played here as a kid. So did several of the other guys."

Alastrine blessed the entrance of the cave and the back tunnel leading out of the main room they were in. They used flint to light a torch so there was some light. They all sat quietly and ate. It was getting late, and they were tired from the long day.

Alastrine had picked men for the watch at two-hour shifts so everyone could get some sleep. In the middle of the third watch, Alastrine was woken by a noise overhead and Will was at his side, whispering that trolls were overhead.

Lance had put the torch out already and started to wake the others, telling them to be quiet and get flat against the wall. Will and Alastrine looked into the darkness and barely made out the figures of trolls and mountain dogs coming down the mountain.

CHAPTER 22

Nonmumi woke with the sun in his eyes. He tried to sit up but was very stiff and sore from the way he had been lying in the boat. On the second attempt, he got himself upright and grabbed the side of the boat as it wobbled.

"Steady," he shouted out loud. "Not in the mood to swim."

The boat slowly stopped rocking, and he took out some jerky and ate as he looked around. All he was seeing was water. Land was way off in the distance. He cursed himself for not putting the anchor down before he passed out. What land was he seeing? Had the boat turned during the night?

"The sun!" he yelled. "The sun comes up in the east." He looked up. It was late morning, but at least he knew the boat had not turned during the night. He turned the boat and started rowing west. He had only rowed for half an hour before he started seeing fishing boats. He rowed up to the closest one. An old fishermen greeted him.

"You look a little bit lost, friend." The old man looked at him and the boat. "Don't usually see a boat this small this far out on the lake."

"I fell asleep in the boat, and it drifted into the water last night," Nonmumi told him. *No need to tell him everything*, he thought to himself.

"I see," the man grunted.

"I just need to get to Vwnrush," Nonmumi continued.

"That's a good bit of rowing," the old man pointed out.

"Yes, well, I can do it. Now how far?"

"Go another five hundred years or so, then start going to your right. You'll see it. It will be late till you get there." He laughed.

"OK, thank you," Nonmumi said as he started to row away.

Nonmumi started thinking to himself that he must not have moved much at all during the night. As he rowed, he thought about Katie again. He hoped he would get to see her. He couldn't believe it, but he still had feelings for her after all these years, and the thought of her made him smile. He followed what the old man had said, and by late evening, he was docking. Nonmumi got out of the boat and was very sore. That was a lot of rowing even for him. He walked very stiff into the downtown part of the city. The city was always busy, this part more so, but not today. Shops were closed, bars were closing, and very few people were out. He stopped a dwarf who was walking by.

"What's going on here?" Nonmumi asked.

"You don't know. The governor has made a curfew because the trolls are coming."

"Have they been seen?"

"Not yet, but word had it that a dwarf trader is bringing them here."

"Really?" Nonmumi was confused.

"Yes, a dwarf named Nonmumi. He turned the chosen ones over to the trolls." The dwarf seemed in a hurry.

"What are you talking about?" Nonmumi demanded.

"Listen, there is a big reward for this dwarf."

Nonmumi was now in shock. How could this be happening?

"You OK?" the dwarf asked him. "Listen, best get inside. Don't want to get caught out after curfew." And the dwarf was gone.

* * * * *

Scott had just come out of his house to catch up with everyone and see how thing were progressing when a boy came running up to him.

"Sir, there is a messenger from Moray here to see you."

"About time. Take me to him." They started off toward the gate.

"Oh, governor, or should I say dictator? Wait, I need to speak to you," came Rosemary's voice behind him. He hung his head; he was hoping not to have to deal with her again today.

"You will have to follow me, Rosemary. I have other things to do," Scott said without looking at her.

"Of course, since the council gave you unchecked power, you are going to ignore your constituents," Rosemary snapped.

Scott stopped. "I have a messenger from Moray waiting for me," he said as he turned and looked at her. "Now if you would like to follow, that would be fine." He turned and started walking again.

"Why, yes, I would like to follow." Rosemary half smiled at him.

Scott picked up the pace, and even the boy was almost running to keep up. When they got to the gate, Rosemary was pretty far behind them. The boy pointed to a young man standing by the guard shack.

"Hi, I'm Scott," he announced, walking over.

"Hi, sir. I'm Dale. I have a message from Alex of Moray." He handed him the sealed envelope. Scott opened it and read it.

"This is not good news," he said as he lowered his hand that held the letter. He looked at Dale. "What are you to do now?"

"Stay and help. My family will be coming soon." Dale smiled.

"I see." Scott put the note in his pocket.

"Don't think I don't know that you were trying to lose me," came Rosemary's voice as she huffed and puffed from trying to keep up with him.

"Rosemary, don't be silly. I know I will never lose you." Scott sighed.

Dale's eyes got big as she approached. He was shocked at her size.

"Dale, this is Rosemary. Her family was involved in starting this city." Scott half smiled, and Dale understood right away that she thought of herself as someone important.

"My family served as the first governor of this city," Rosemary corrected him.

"Yes, they did." Scott smiled at her.

"Now may I have a minute of your time?" Rosemary was smug with him.

"Of course. What can I do for you?"

"My mother said that I should help out somehow, that everyone is giving and I need to do the same, that giving would make me feel good." Rosemary was waving her hand in the air as she was talking, and you could tell she didn't believe anything she was saying.

"I see, and what is it that you want to give?" Scott could hardly wait to hear this answer.

"Scott, good, there you are," Jimmy said as he came up to him.

Jimmy was the man who was working off the walls to make them stronger. He was tall and built like a brick house. His hands were rough from working with them all his life. He was a gentle soul who always had a kind word for anyone he met.

"Just a minute, Rosemary. What is it, Jimmy?" Scott said, holding a finger up in front of Rosemary. He enjoyed that as he knew it made Rosemary mad.

"The walls are coming along good, but there is something you need to come see."

"OK, let's go then. Dale, you can follow. I'll have you work with me until you family gets here."

"Excuse me, I was talking." Rosemary stomped her foot.

"Please follow me and talk," Scott said.

They all follow Jimmy. It was Jimmy, Scott, Dale, and Rosemary bringing up the rear.

"As I was saying, my mother thinks I should help out."

"And what is it you want to do?" Scott asked.

"Well, I don't want to have to touch them or anything like that." Rosemary made a sour face.

"Of course not." Scott rolled his eyes.

They started up the stairs that lead to the top of the wall. Scott thought, for sure Rosemary would not follow, but she did. The stairs made noise and sagged a little as she was climbing them, and they all said a prayer to the goddess.

"So I was thinking, maybe I could donate some of my clothes."

"Really? That would be nice," Scott said, not sure what else to say to that.

"That's is what I thought, but my mother said I need to give some time. Some of my time. Can you believe that?"

They were on the wall now, walking to where the gate was below them. The walkway wasn't narrow, but for Rosemary, it was and they all just kept praying.

"Well, we can use all the help we can get," Scott said.

"There." Jimmy pointed as they cleared the trees that had been blocking their view.

Scott's mouth dropped open when he saw what Jimmy was pointing to. Hundreds, maybe thousands, of people coming in, some on boats from Perth, most likely on foot carrying everything they could. Livestock was following most of them. Children crying from being tired of walking and traveling. All covered in dust and dirt from days of being on the road, and even at this distance, he could see the despair in their faces.

"Oh my" was all even Rosemary could say.

"I sent scouts out on horses, and they say this goes on for miles," Jimmy said.

"I don't think I could be much help here," Rosemary said softly and turned to walk away.

"I am nowhere near prepared for this. I can use all the help I can get," Scott said with tears filling his eyes as Rosemary kept walking slowly away.

About the Author

Donald L. Marino was born in central Pennsylvania. As a senior in high school, Donald wrote his first book, a *Hardy Boys* style that got him an A in English class. Donald spent four years in the Army, where he lived in Germany and was in the first Gulf War. Since coming home, he moved to northeast Pennsylvania where Donald was involved with community theater for over twelve years and also took an improved class in New York. Donald married his husband, Anthony, and took his last name, Marino. Donald loves going to Rehoboth with his husband but also loves sitting at home and writing. Donald loves to write because it gives him a chance to be creative. He loves the challenge of figuring out plots and how to make them work. Donald's favorite author is Terry Brooks.

CPSIA information can be obtained
at www.ICGtesting.com
Printed in the USA
BVHW03s0935260718
522459BV00002B/7/P